☜ **W9-AOU-711**

EMIL AND THE

DETECTIVES

A NOVEL FOR CHILDREN

Erich Kästner

Translated by W. Martin

Illustrations by Walter Trier

Introduction by Maurice Sendak

THE OVERLOOK PRESS
New York, NY

This edition first published in paperback in the United States in 2014 by
The Overlook Press, Peter Mayer Publishers, Inc.

141 Wooster Street
New York, NY 10012
www.overlookpress.com

For bulk and special sales, please contact sales@overlookny.com,
or write us at the above address.

Cataloging-in-Publication Data is available from the Library of Congress

Book design and type formatting by Bernard Schleifer
Manufactured in the United States of America
ISBN 978-1-4683-0829-7
10 9 8 7 6 5 4 3 2

INTRODUCTION
MAURICE SENDAK

EMIL IS A WONDER—*WAS* A WONDER WHEN I FIRST MADE HIS acquaintance several years after he was published in America. I was about ten at the time. I don't remember other books from that period of my life, except, for special reasons, *Mickey Mouse in Pygmy Land* and *The Prince and the Pauper*. But the very title *Emil and the Detectives* conjures up for me a grab bag of delicious memories: the thrill of Emil's adventures; the vivid sense of the city of Berlin, where most of the action takes place; the story's real danger and playful comedy and total lack of condescension. This wasn't "a boy's book" spoiled by a mincing writer endearing himself to a bunch of little quibblers. I've never forgotten that imagined smell of Berlin, or the city kids who help Emil out with his very serious problem, or the fascinating people, even eccentric people! Emil's cousin, Pony, forever on her bicycle, is still my favorite character.

   Emil and the Detectives was first published in Germany in 1929; an American edition followed the next year. I probably met up with Emil in 1938 and it was love at first sight. Erich Kästner's madcap mystery, with its intriguing title, had been presented to me by my sister, who was hopelessly hooked on books and wanted me and my brother to be equally addicted. This book was a golden object, only for me, my book. Since it had been chosen by my sister, it had to be something very worth reading, something different and new.

By 1938 the dread of war and all things German filled my family's life with despair. "On November 10, 1938," as Kästner himself recorded, "gangs of men wearing black breeches, riding boots, and civilian jackets smashed Jewish store windows with iron rods." This happened in Berlin, *Emil*'s city, and is infamously memorialized as Crystal Night. Before that terrible event, in 1933, all of Kästner's books (except for *Emil*!!) were burned in a large square next to the Berlin opera house, the square crowded with approving onlookers. Kästner was there.

How could I read *Emil and the Detectives* without a heavy sense of guilt? But the book had, and still has, the opposite effect of making me feel part of Emil's little gang of boys, all of them out to help Emil find his stolen money. Here we see steadfastness, the loyalty of small children working together and achieving success by simply believing in each other. Here is the essence of boyhood, with all its endearing human quirkiness.

Emil is a little masterpiece. It shows us the heroic nature of children, how they can stick together and accomplish wonders without the help of the inept grownups. What a marvelous gift! Read it and you will be happy.

It is very funny, too.

—MAURICE SENDAK

EMIL AND THE DETECTIVES

FIRST OF ALL

EMIL HIMSELF

This is, first things being first, Emil himself. In his navy-blue Sunday suit. He doesn't like wearing it, and only puts it on when he has to. Blue suits get stained so easily. And then Emil's mother dampens the clothes brush, clamps her son between her knees, and brushes him down, all the while scolding him, "Emil, Emil! You know perfectly well I can't afford to get you another suit." And once again he remembers—too late—how she works all day to put food on the table and so he can go to school.

SECOND OF ALL

MRS. TABLETOE THE HAIRDRESSER, EMIL'S MOM

When Emil was five years old, his father, Mr. Tabletoe, the master plumber, passed away. Since then, Mrs. Tabletoe cuts hair. And gives perms. And washes the hair of the neighborhood housewives and salesclerks. Besides that, she has to cook, keep the house clean, and take care of all the laundry all by herself. She loves Emil more than anything, and she's glad she can work and make money. Sometimes she sings funny songs. Sometimes she gets sick, and then Emil makes fried eggs sunnyside-up for her. That's something he's good at. He can cook hamburger, too. With softened bread and onion.

THIRD OF ALL

A PRETTY FANCY TRAIN COMPARTMENT

This compartment is part of a train bound for Berlin. I suppose it's safe to say that strange things will occur in this compartment, already in the next few chapters. Train compartments are odd affairs to begin with. Complete strangers find themselves together here and after a few hours know each other so well, it's as if they've been friends for years. Sometimes that's all very nice and completely normal. Sometimes, however, it's not. After all, who knows who those people are?

FOURTH OF ALL

THE MAN IN THE BOWLER HAT

Nobody knows him. They say you should always assume the best about people until they've proven themselves to be otherwise. But I'd like to urge you all to be on your guard around this guy. As they say, an ounce of prevention is worth a pound of cure. Humans are fundamentally good, they say. And that may well be true. But you can't make it too easy on them, those good humans. Otherwise they might go bad all of a sudden.

FIFTH OF ALL

PONY THE HAT,
EMIL'S COUSIN

This little girl on the bike is Emil's cousin from Berlin. Some people insist that a cousin can be any distant relative, and that for the sake of precision I should introduce her as Emil's first cousin. I don't know what it's like in your family, but I call all my cousins—first, second, even third—simply "cousin," and it's no different with the Tabletoes. Of course, if people don't like it, they're free to take a pencil and insert the word "first" over or under "cousin." I'm not going to argue about it. In any case, Pony the Hat is a charming girl and that's not her real name. Her mother and Mrs. Tabletoe are sisters. Pony the Hat is just a nickname.

Sixth of All

THE HOTEL ON
NOLLENDORF SQUARE

Nollendorf Square is in Berlin. And right on Nollendorf
Square, if I'm not mistaken, is the hotel where various
people in this story come together without ever actually
meeting. But it could just as well be on Wittenberg Place.
Or even on Fehrbellin Place. Which is to say: I know
exactly where it is, but the hotel manager came to me
when he heard I was planning to write a book about this
business, and asked me not to mention the address. It
would hardly be good publicity for his hotel if it got
around that "those kinds" of people stayed there. I told
him that was fine with me. And he went on his way.

SEVENTH OF ALL

THE BOY WITH THE
BICYCLE HORN

His name is Gustav, or Gus for short. And he has the best grades in gym. What else does he have? A pretty good heart and a bicycle horn. All the kids in the neighborhood know him and treat him like he was their president. When he runs through the courtyards honking his horn, the boys drop everything, plunge down the stairs, and ask him what's happening. Mostly he's just drumming up a couple of teams for a soccer game, and they all go off to the playground. But sometimes the bicycle horn has other uses. Like now, in this situation with Emil.

EIGHTH OF ALL

THE BANK BRANCH OFFICE

In every neighborhood the large banks have their branch offices. If you have the money, you can commission the purchase of stocks there; and if you have an account, you can withdraw cash. You can cash checks there, too, as long as they're not "for deposit only." Sometimes sales-clerks and assistants come by to change a ten-mark bill into hundreds of smaller coins so their cashier will have something to make change with. And if someone wants to convert dollars or Swiss francs or liras into German money, they can do that here, too. Even at night, some-times, people come to the bank. Even though there's no one there to help them. So they help themselves instead.

NINTH OF ALL

EMIL'S GRANDMA

She's the most upbeat grandmother I've ever met. Despite the fact that all she's had her whole life long is trouble. For some people it isn't hard at all to be in a good mood. For others, it's serious, difficult business. Back in the day, Emil's grandmother lived with his parents. But when Mr. Tabletoe the master plumber passed away, she went to live with her other daughter in Berlin. Emil's mother didn't earn enough to support three people. Now the old woman lives in Berlin. And every letter she writes ends with the words, "I'm doing fine and I hope the same for you."

Tenth of All

THE CASE ROOM OF A MAJOR NEWSPAPER

Everything that happens turns up in the news. It just has to be a little unusual. When a calf is born with four legs, that's not so interesting, of course. But when it has five or six—and it happens!—then the grownups like to read about it over breakfast. When Mr. Mueller is an upstanding citizen, no one particularly cares. But when Mr. Mueller puts water in the milk and goes selling it as half-and-half, then he's sure to find himself in the paper. No matter what he does. Have you ever walked by a newspaper building at night? You can hear it ringing and tapping and clattering inside, and the wall shakes.

So, now we can finally start!

CHAPTER ONE

EMIL HELPS WASH HAIR

"AND," SAID MRS. TABLETOE, "DON'T FORGET TO BRING that pitcher of warm water with you." She had already grabbed the other pitcher and the little blue tub of chamomile shampoo and was walking from the kitchen into the living room. Emil grabbed his pitcher and walked out after his mom.

In the living room a woman was sitting with her head leaned back over the white sink. Her hair was untied and hung down like a lot of loose knitting yarn. Emil's mother poured the chamomile shampoo into the blonde hair and began lathering the woman's head.

"Is it too hot?" she asked.

"No, it's fine," the head answered.

"Oh, it's Mrs. Worth, the baker's wife! Hello there!" said Emil and set down his pitcher under the wash-stand.

"Aren't you lucky, Emil. I hear you're going to Berlin," said the head. It sounded like someone talking from under a pile of whipped cream.

"He didn't really want to go at first," said Emil's mother as she scrubbed the baker's wife's scalp. "But why should the boy spend his vacation here, boring himself to death? He doesn't know Berlin at all. And my sister Martha has been trying to get us to come for years. Her husband has a good paying job. He works for the post office. A desk job. Of course I can't go with him. There's too much to do before the holidays. But, well, he's a big boy. He'll just have to be careful on the train is all. Anyway, my mother is picking him up at Frederick Street Station. They're meeting in front of the flower shop."

"I'm sure he'll like Berlin. It's a great place for kids. We were there with our bowling league a year ago. It was so busy! They have streets there that really are as bright at night as they are during the day. And you should have seen the cars!" Mrs. Worth exclaimed from inside the sink.

"Are there a lot of foreign cars there?" asked Emil.

"How would I know?" said Mrs. Worth and started to sneeze. The soapsuds had gotten into her nose.

"Listen you, you'd better get ready," Emil's mother said to him. "I laid out your good suit in the bedroom. Go put it on now so we can eat lunch when I'm finished doing Mrs. Worth's hair."

"What shirt should I wear?" asked Emil.

"It's all out on the bed. And don't rip your socks when you put them on. And make sure you wash up first. And put new shoelaces in the shoes. Shake a leg!"

"Oh heck," remarked Emil, and strolled off.

Once Mrs. Worth had gotten her permanent, admired it in the mirror, and left, Emil's mother went to the bedroom and found Emil walking around with a frown on his face.

"Could you please tell me who invented the good suit?

"I have no idea. Why do you want to know?"

"Give me his address and I'll shoot the man!"

"Oh, you poor boy! And to think of all those other kids who are sad because they don't even have a good suit. I suppose we all have our troubles . . . Oh, before I forget, ask Aunt Martha to iron it for you tonight, and make sure to hang it up on a hanger. Do me a favor and brush it off first, though. Then tomorrow you can wear your cardigan again, your army jacket. Anything else? Your suitcase is packed. The flowers for Aunt Martha are wrapped up. I'll give you the money for Grandma later. And now, young man, we should have some lunch." Mrs. Tabletoe put her arm around Emil's shoulders and transported him into the kitchen.

They had macaroni and ham with grated parmesan cheese. Emil gobbled it down like a machine. Except every now and then he stopped and looked over at his mom as if he were afraid that, with him leaving so soon, she might be offended by his eating so much.

"Write me as soon as you get there. I packed a post-card. It's in the suitcase, right on top."

"No problem," said Emil, pushing a piece of macaroni off his knee as discreetly as possible. Luckily his mom didn't notice a thing.

"And give everyone my love. And keep your head on your shoulders. People in Berlin are different than they are here in New Town. On Sunday Uncle Robert will take you to the Bode Museum. So behave yourself. I don't want people thinking we have no manners here."

"You have my word of honor," said Emil.

After they ate, they went back into the living room. Mom pulled a tin box from the cabinet and counted the money in it. She shook her head and counted it again. Then she asked, "Who was here yesterday afternoon, do you remember?"

"Miss Thomas," Emil said, "and Mrs. Homburg."

"Right. But it's still off." She thought for a moment, looked for the piece of paper with her earnings written down on it, added them up, and said at last, "I'm missing eight marks."

"The gas man was here this morning."

"Of course! Then this is the correct amount, unfortunately." Emil's mother let out a whistle, presumably to vent her troubles, then she pulled three bills out of the tin box. "Emil, here's a hundred and forty marks. One hundred mark bill and two twenties. Give a hundred twenty to Grandma and tell her I'm sorry I didn't send anything last time. I just didn't have enough. So instead I'm giving it to you to give to her. And more than usual. Give her a kiss for me, too. All right? The other twenty is for you.

Use it to buy your ticket back. It should come to ten marks. I don't know the exact amount. The rest is for you to use when you all go out, to pay for what you eat and drink. Well, it's always good to have a few extra marks in your pocket just in case. So, here's the envelope from Aunt Martha's letter. I'll put the money in here. Just make sure you don't lose it! Where will you keep it?"

She put the three bills into the envelope, which had been slit open along its length, folded it in half, and handed it to Emil.

He thought for a moment, then slipped the envelope into his right inside pocket, deep down, patted the outside of his blue suit coat to make sure, and said confidently, "Well, it's not going anywhere now."

"And don't tell anyone in the train how much money you have on you!"

"Mom!" Emil was deeply insulted. To think he could do something so stupid!

Mrs. Tabletoe added a little money to her wallet. Then she brought the tin box back to the cupboard and took another look at the letter from her sister in Berlin, which listed the exact departure and arrival times for Emil's train . . .

Some of you are no doubt thinking that there's no point in having such a long talk, like the one Mrs. Tabletoe the hairdresser just had with her son, over a mere hundred and forty marks. And for people who make two thousand or twenty thousand or even a hundred thousand marks a month, there certainly wouldn't be.

But in case you haven't heard, most people earn much, much less. Whether you like it or not, anyone who makes thirty-five marks a week has to consider the hundred and forty marks that he or she has saved up to be a lot of money. For the vast majority of people, a hundred marks is practically as good as a million; an extra three or six or seven zeroes hardly makes a difference. Even in their dreams they couldn't imagine how much a million is really worth.

Emil no longer had a father. So his mother had a lot to do. She worked as a hairdresser in her living-room salon, washing blonde hair and brown. She worked long hours to make sure they had food on the table and could pay not only for the gas, electricity, and rent, but for clothes, books, and school fees, too. Sometimes, though, she got sick and had to stay in bed. The doctor came and prescribed medicine, and Emil prepared hot compresses for her and cooked in the kitchen for the two of them. When she was asleep, he even mopped the floor with a wet rag so she wouldn't say, "I should get up. The house is a mess."

Would you understand what I meant, and not laugh, if I told you that Emil was a momma's boy?

You see, he really loved his mom. He would have died of shame if he caught himself being lazy while she worked and counted every penny and kept on working. So imagine if he stopped doing his homework or started copying off of Richard Naumann. Imagine him going out of his way to skip school. He saw what she went through to make sure he had everything the other students had. So just imagine him lying to her and making her worry.

Emil was a momma's boy. It's true. But he wasn't the type that can't help being that way because they're cowards and selfish and not really kids at all. He was a momma's boy because he wanted to be one. He had made a resolution, the way you make a resolution to stop going to the movies or eating candy. He made a resolution, and it wasn't always easy to keep it.

But when he came home at Easter break and could say, "Look at my report card, Mom. Straight A's again!" then he knew it was worth it. He enjoyed the praise he got at school and everywhere else, not for his own sake, but because it made Mom happy. He was proud that in his own way he could pay back even a little of what she had tirelessly given him her whole life . . .

"Goodness!" cried Emil's mom, "we have to get to the station. It's a quarter past one already, and the train leaves shortly before two."

"Then let's get going, Mrs. Tabletoe!" said Emil to his mom. "But, just so you know, I'm carrying the suitcase myself!"

CHAPTER TWO

OFFICER JESCHKE DOESN'T SAY ANYTHING

OUT IN FRONT OF THE HOUSE EMIL'S MOM SAID, "IF A HORSE-drawn comes, then we'll ride to the station."

Do any of you know what a horse-drawn streetcar looks like? Well, now that one is coming around the corner and just stopped because Emil waved it down, I guess I'll have to describe it for you. But quickly, before it trundles off again.

A horse-drawn streetcar is, first of all, an amazing thing. Second of all, it runs on rails, just like a real, grown-up streetcar, and its cars look almost the same. The only difference is that it has a horse harnessed to it. Emil and his friends thought the horse-drawn was an outrage. They dreamed of an electric train with upper and lower decks and five headlights in front and three in back. But New Town's city council felt that the town's four miles of track could be handled well enough by living horsepower. So no one was even thinking of electricity yet, and the driver didn't have to deal with all sorts of cranks and levers. All he had to do was hold the reins in his left hand and the whip in his right. Giddy-up!

And if the person who lived at 12 Town Hall Street was in the horse-drawn and wanted to get out, he or she simply knocked on the glass pane. Then the driver said "Whoa!" and the passenger was home. The real streetcar stop was probably somewhere in front of house number 30 or 46. But the New Town Streetcar Co. didn't much care. It had time. The horse had time. The driver had time. New Town's inhabitants had time. And if people were really in a hurry, they went on foot . . .

Mrs. Tabletoe and her son got out on the square in front of the train station. As Emil was fishing his suitcase down from the top of the streetcar, a deep voice rumbled behind them, "So, off on a trip to Switzerland, are you?"

It was Officer Jeschke the police chief. Emil's mom answered, "No, my son is going for a week to Berlin to visit his relatives." Emil suddenly felt the blood rush to his face, for he had a very guilty conscience. Recently, after they had gym class in the field by the river, he and a dozen kids went up to the statue of Grand Duke Charles, who was known as Crooked Cheek Charles, and slyly placed an old hat on his cold stone head. Then, because he could draw so well, Emil was lifted up by the others in order to draw a red nose and a tar-black moustache on the Grand

Duke's face with colored markers. Then, while he was still drawing, Officer Jeschke appeared at the other end of the main square!

They all scattered like lightning. But of course he might have recognized them.

But he didn't say anything. Instead he just told Emil to have a good trip and asked Emil's mother how she was getting on and how business was going.

Emil still had a bad feeling, though. And as he was hauling his suitcase across the empty square to the station, his knees felt wobbly. He expected Jeschke to shout after him any minute, "Emil Tabletoe, you're under arrest! Hands up!" But nothing happened. Maybe the policeman was simply waiting until Emil got back?

Then Emil's mother went to the counter and bought the train ticket (third class, of course) and a platform ticket. Then they went to Platform 1—New Town has four platforms, I'll have you know—and waited there for the train to Berlin. Only a few minutes were left. "Don't forget anything, dear! And don't sit on the flowers! Have someone help you put the suitcase up on the luggage rack. But be polite and say please!"

"I can get the suitcase up there myself. I'm not made of cardboard, you know."

"Fine. But don't forget to get off the train. You arrive at 6:17 p.m. at Frederick Street Station. Make sure you don't get out before then, at Zoo Station or any of the others!"

"Have no fear, young lady!"

"And don't be a smart-aleck with other people like you are with your mother! And don't leave the wax paper I wrapped your sandwiches in on the floor. And don't lose the money!"

Panicked, Emil clutched his suit jacket and checked the right inside pocket. Then he gave a sigh of relief and said, "All hands on deck!" He took his mother's arm and walked with her down the platform and back.

"And you, don't overwork yourself, Mom! And don't get sick! There'd be no one there to take care of you. I'd hop on the first airplane, though, and come home. And you should write to me, too. I'm not staying any more than a week, though, just so you know." He gave his mom a hug, and she gave him a kiss on the nose.

Then the passenger train to Berlin pulled in, screeching and hissing, and came to a stop. Emil gave his mother another hug. Then he climbed up with his suitcase into a compartment. His mother handed the bouquet of flowers to him and the bag of sandwiches and asked if he had found a seat. He nodded.

"Remember to get out at Frederick Street!"

He nodded.

"Grandma will be waiting for you in front of the flower shop."

He nodded.

"And behave yourself, you rascal!"

He nodded.

"And be nice to Pony the Hat. You'll hardly recognize each other."

He nodded.

"And write to me."

"Okay. You write, too."

It could have gone on like that for hours if it weren't for the train schedule. The conductor with the little red bag called out, "All aboard! All aboard!" The train doors clapped shut. The engine lurched forward. And off they went.

Emil's mom waved her handkerchief until the train was out of sight. Then she turned around and went home. And since she was holding her handkerchief anyway, she cried a little, too.

But not for long. Because at home Mrs. Augustin the butcher's wife was already sitting in the living room, waiting to have her hair shampooed.

CHAPTER THREE

THE TRIP TO BERLIN
CAN BEGIN

EMIL TOOK OFF HIS CAP AND SAID, "GOOD AFTERNOON
everyone. Are any of these seats free?"

Of course there was a free seat. A heavyset woman,
who had taken off her left shoe because it pinched, said to
the man next to her, who wheezed horribly every time he
breathed, "Children with manners like that are so rare
these days. When I think back on my childhood . . .
Goodness! Was the world ever different then!" As she
talked, she would clench then release her crushed toes in
her left stocking. Emil watched with interest. The man
could hardly nod from all his wheezing.

Emil was already familiar with those people who
always say, "Goodness, everything was better in the old
days." And he no longer listened when people told him
that in the old days the air was cleaner or that cows had
bigger heads. Because it usually wasn't true. Those people

simply wanted to be dissatisfied, because otherwise they would have to be satisfied.

He patted the right side of his suit coat and was relieved to hear the envelope rustling in its pocket. The other passengers all looked fairly trustworthy, hardly like robbers or murderers. Next to the man with the wheezing problem sat a woman knitting a scarf. At the window, next to Emil, a gentleman in a bowler hat was reading the newspaper.

Suddenly the man in the bowler put his paper down, pulled a bar of chocolate from his pocket, held it out to the boy and said, "Well, young man, how about some?"

"Don't mind if I do," replied Emil and took the chocolate. Then as an afterthought, he quickly took off his cap, bowed a little, and said, "Allow me to introduce myself. I'm Emil Tabletoe."

The other passengers all smiled, and the gentleman ceremoniously lifted his bowler and said, "Pleased to meet you. My name is Groundsnow."

Then the fat woman who had taken off her shoe asked, "Does a Mr. Squatneck who sells drapes still live in New Town?"

"Of course Mr. Squatneck lives there," Emil told her. "Do you know him? He just bought the property his store is on."

"Well, say hello to him from Mrs. Jacob from Great Greenow."

"But I'm on my way to Berlin."

"Well it can wait until you get back," said Mrs. Jacob, wiggling her toes and chuckling until her hat slipped down onto her forehead.

"So, you're going to Berlin, are you?" said Mr. Groundsnow.

"That's right! My grandmother is waiting for me by the flower shop at Frederick Street Station," replied Emil. He patted his jacket again, and the envelope rustled. Thank God, it was still there!

"So, have you been to Berlin before?"

"No."

"Well, you're in for a big surprise. In Berlin they have buildings now that are a hundred floors high. They have to fasten the roofs to the sky to keep them from blowing away . . .

"And if you're in a hurry to get to another part of town, you just have yourself packed in a box at the post office, dropped into a pneumatic tube, and shot straight to the post office in whatever neighborhood you're going to . . .

"And when you're broke, you can go to the bank, leave your brain there as collateral, and get a thousand marks. People can only live without their brain for two days, and you only get it back when you've given them twelve hundred marks in return. It's amazing what surgical equipment can do these days . . ."

"It looks like you left your brain at the bank as well,"

said the man with the wheezing problem to the man in the bowler. Then he added, "Stop the nonsense already."

Fat Mrs. Jacob stopped wiggling her toes out of fear. And the other woman put her knitting down.

Emil gave out a forced laugh. The two men started to argue. Emil thought, "Like I care!" and unpacked his salami sandwiches, although he had only just had lunch. As he was working on the third sandwich, the train came to a halt at a huge station. Emil couldn't see the sign for the station, and he didn't understand what the conductor was yelling outside the window. Almost all the other passengers got out—the wheezing man, the knitting woman, and even Mrs. Jacob. She had a hard time getting her shoe back on and almost didn't make it out the door.

"Say hello to Mr. Squatneck for me," she said on the way out.

Emil nodded.

Then he and the man in the bowler hat were by themselves. Emil wasn't all too happy about that. A man who gives out chocolate and tells outlandish stories is pretty weird. Emil wanted to pat his suit coat, to check on the envelope, but he didn't dare. Instead, after the train started up again, he went to the washroom, and there he pulled the envelope from his pocket, counted the money— it was still all there—and really didn't know what to do.

Finally he had an idea. He found a pin in the lapel of his jacket, stuck it through the three bills, then through the envelope, and then through the suit lining. He had

pinned his money down, so to speak. Well then, he thought, nothing can happen to it now. And he went back to the compartment.

Mr. Groundsnow had made himself at home in a corner and was sleeping. Emil was happy he didn't have to make conversation, and he looked out the window. Trees, windmills, fields, factories, herds of cows, and waving farmers all passed by outside. It was beautiful to look at, how everything spun around again and again, almost like on a turntable. But you can't spend all day looking through the window.

Mr. Groundsnow continued to sleep and snored a little. Emil would have liked nothing more than to get up and pace back and forth, but then his fellow traveler would have woken up, and that was the last thing he wanted. So he leaned back in the opposite corner of the compartment and observed the sleeping man. Why didn't the guy ever take his hat off, Emil wondered. He had a long face, a pencil-thin, black moustache, and hundreds of wrinkles around his mouth. His ears were as thin as paper and stuck straight out.

Yikes! Emil started with fright. He had almost dozed off! And sleeping was entirely out of the question. If only someone else were there in the compartment. Although the train had stopped a few times, no one came in. But it was only four o'clock, and Emil still had two more hours to go. He pinched his leg. That always helped when he was in Mr. Bremser's history class in school.

It worked for a while. Emil thought about how Pony the Hat must look now. But he couldn't picture her face any more. All he remembered was that the last time they saw each other—when she and Grandma and Aunt Martha were visiting New Town—she had wanted to box with him. He had refused, of course, because she was a featherweight and he was at least a light heavyweight. It would be unfair, he told her. What if he plastered her with an uppercut? They'd have to peel her down from the wall afterwards.

But she only stopped insisting on a match when Aunt Martha stepped in.

Whoa! He almost fell off the seat. Dozing off again? He kept pinching his legs. He probably had black and blue marks all over. But it was of no use.

He tried counting buttons. He counted downwards from the top and then upwards from the bottom. Top to bottom there were twenty-three buttons. But bottom to top there were twenty-four. Emil leaned back and tried to figure out how that happened.

And while he was at it, he fell asleep.

CHAPTER FOUR

A Dream in Which There's a Lot of Running

SUDDENLY EMIL HAD THE FEELING THAT THE TRAIN WAS going in spirals, like the toy train sets that kids play with in their rooms. He looked out the window and found it all very strange. The spiral kept getting smaller. The engine kept coming closer to the caboose, and it looked like it was doing it on purpose! The train was running in circles like a dog trying to bite its own tail. And there in the middle of that furious black circle stood trees and a windmill made of glass and a towering skyscraper two hundred floors high.

Emil wanted to check the time and started to take his watch out of his pocket. He pulled and pulled on the chain, but what came out was Mom's grandfather clock from the living room. He looked at the face and the time read "115 miles per hour. Danger! Spitting on the floor prohibited on penalty of death!" He looked out the window again. The engine was drawing even closer to the caboose. And he was terrified, because if the engine ran into the caboose there would be a train wreck. That much was clear. And Emil had no interest in waiting around until it happened. He opened the door and ran down the sideboard. Maybe the engineer had fallen asleep? Emil peered into the compartment windows as he clambered forward. There was no one inside. The train was empty. Emil saw only one person, a man with a bowler hat made of chocolate. The man broke off part of the brim and ate it. Emil knocked on his window and pointed at the engine. But the man only laughed, broke off another piece of chocolate, and rubbed his belly because it tasted so good.

Finally Emil made it to the coal car. He nimbly monkey-barred his way up to the engineer, who was sitting on a coach seat, brandishing his whip and holding the reins as if the train were being pulled by a team of horses. And as a matter of fact, it was! Three rows of three horses each were pulling the train. They had silver rollerskates on their hoofs and were gliding on them down the rails, singing, "M errily merrily merrily merrily, life is but a dream."

Emil shook the coachman and shouted, "Pull up the horses! We're about to crash!" Then he saw that the coachman was none other than Officer Jeschke. The man glared at him and yelled, "Who were the other boys? Who defaced the Grand Duke?"

"I did it!" said Emil.

"Who else?"

"I'm not saying!"

"Then we'll just have to keep going in circles!"

Officer Jeschke cracked the whip so that his horses reared up and took off even faster than before after the caboose. And there at the back of the caboose was Mrs. Jacob, waving her shoes around, visibly terrified of the horses, who were snapping at her toes.

"I'll give you twenty marks, Officer Jeschke!" cried Emil. "Pipe down, will you!" shouted Jeschke and began whipping his horses like a madman.

Emil couldn't take it any longer and jumped off the train. He turned twenty somersaults down the hill, but made it without a scratch. He stood up and looked around for the train. While he was standing there like that, all nine horses turned their heads toward him. Officer Jeschke had jumped up and was thrashing them with his whip, roaring, "Giddy up! Follow him!" The horses leaped off the rails and charged at Emil, the cars bouncing after them like rubber balls.

Emil didn't stop to think, he simply ran off as fast as his legs could carry him. Across a field, past a great number of trees, and through a creek toward the sky-scraper. Now and then he looked back. The train thundered after him without letting up. It flattened the trees and broke them to splinters. Only one tree, an enormous oak, was left standing, and there in its highest branches sat fat Mrs. Jacob, swaying in the wind, cry-

ing and trying in vain to get her shoe back on. Emil kept running.

The two-hundred-floor-high skyscraper had a large, black door. He ran in it and through the building and out the other side. The train came after him. Emil would have liked nothing more than to sit down in a corner and fall asleep, he was so awfully tired, his whole body was shaking with exhaustion. But he couldn't doze off! The train was already clattering through the skyscraper.

Emil saw an iron ladder running up the side of the skyscraper to the top. He started climbing up. Luckily he was a good athlete. As he was climbing, he counted the floors. At the fiftieth floor he actually turned and looked down. The trees had gotten extremely small, and the glass windmill was hardly recognizable. But—no! The train was driving up the side of the building! Emil kept climbing higher and higher. And the train stomped and roared up the ladder as if it were a train track.

The 100th floor, the 120th floor, 140th, 160th, 180th, the 200th floor! Emil stood on the roof and had no idea what he should do next. He could already hear the horses' neighing. So the boy ran across the roof to the opposite end, pulled his handkerchief from his suit, and unfolded it. And just as the sweating horses came climbing over the parapet with the train in tow, Emil held his unfurled handkerchief over his head and jumped off. He heard the train knocking over the chimneys behind him. Then for a while he neither heard nor saw anything at all.

And then he landed with a thud. Boom! He was in a field.

At first he just lay there, exhausted, his eyes closed, and wanted nothing more than to drift into a pleasant dream. But he didn't feel entirely safe yet, so he looked up at the skyscraper and saw the nine horses up on top opening umbrellas. Officer Jeschke had an umbrella, too, and was using it to prod the horses. They sat up on their hind legs, hopped forward a little, and jumped into the air. And now the train was sailing down toward the field, growing larger and larger.

Emil jumped to his feet again and took off across the field toward the glass windmill. It was translucent, and he saw his mother inside, shampooing Mrs. Augustin's hair. Thank God, he thought, and ran into the windmill through the back door.

"Mom!" he yelled. "What should I do?"

"What's wrong, dear?" his mother asked, and went on shampooing.

"Look out the wall!"

Mrs. Tabletoe looked out and saw the horses and train land on the field and charge off toward the windmill.

"Why, it's Officer Jeschke," said Emil's mom, and shook her head in amazement.

"He's been racing after me like a madman all day!"

"Is that so?"

"A few days ago I was on the main square, and I painted a red nose and a moustache on the face of Grand

Duke Charles with the crooked cheek."

"Well, where else where you supposed to put the moustache?" said Mrs. Augustin with a snort.

"Nowhere, Mrs. Augustin. But that's not the worst of it. He wanted to know who else was there with me. But I can't tell him that. It's a question of honor."

"Emil's got a point," said his mother. "But what do we do now?"

"Why not simply turn on the motor, Mrs. Tabletoe?" said Mrs. Augustin.

Emil's mom pulled down a lever on the table, and the windmill's four sails began to turn. Because they were made of glass and the sun was shining, they gleamed and shimmered so much that you could hardly look at them. When the nine horses and their train came running up, they got spooked, reared up on their hind legs, and refused to go a step further. Officer Jeschke swore so loudly you could hear it through the glass walls. But the horses wouldn't budge.

"There. Now would you please continue shampooing my scalp?" said Mrs. Augustin, "Your boy has nothing to worry about now."

So Mrs. Tabletoe the hairdresser got back to work. Emil sat down on a chair, which was made of glass as well, and let out a whistle. Then he laughed and said, "Well that's just great. If I'd known you were here, I wouldn't have bothered climbing up that darn skyscraper."

"I hope you didn't tear your suit!" said his mom.

Then she asked, "Did you keep your eye on the money?"

At that, Emil felt a sudden jolt and fell off the glass chair with a loud crash.

And woke up.

CHAPTER FIVE

EMIL GETS OFF AT THE
WRONG STATION

THE TRAIN WAS JUST STARTING TO MOVE AGAIN WHEN HE woke up. He had fallen off the seat while he was sleeping and now lay on the floor in a state of shock. But he still didn't know exactly why. His heart was pounding like a jackhammer. There he was, sitting in a train, and he had practically forgotten how he'd gotten there. Gradually it all came back to him. Right—he was on his way to Berlin. And he'd fallen asleep. Just like the man in the bowler hat . . .

All of a sudden Emil sat bolt upright and gasped, "He's gone!" His knees started shaking. Slowly, deliberately, he stood up and mechanically patted down his suit. Then came the next question: Is the money still there? It was a question he was almost too scared to ask.

For a long time he stood leaning against the door without daring to move. That man Groundsnow had been sitting right over there, sleeping and snoring. And now he was gone. Of course, nothing at all might have happened. Actually, it was silly to fear the worst, first thing. He couldn't expect the whole world to be traveling to Frederick Street Station in Berlin just because he was. And no doubt the money was right where he'd left it. First of all, it was in his pocket. Second, it was in an envelope. And third, he'd fastened it with a pin to the lining. Slowly he reached into the right inside pocket . . .

The pocket was empty! The money was gone!

Emil rummaged through the pocket with his left hand. He patted and squeezed the front of the jacket with his right. But it didn't help. The pocket was empty, and the money was gone.

"Ouch!" Emil pulled his hand out of the pocket, and along with it the pin he'd stuck through the money. Nothing was left but that pin. And now it was stuck in his left index finger, making it bleed.

He wrapped his handkerchief around the finger and cried. Not because of a few ridiculous drops of blood, of course. Fourteen days ago Emil had run into a street light, almost knocking it over, and he still had a bump on his forehead. But he didn't cry for a second over that.

He was crying because of the money. And he was crying because of his mother. And if you don't understand why, no matter how tough you may think you are, then you're beyond help. Emil knew how his mother had slaved away for months in order to save up the hundred and forty marks for his grandmother and to send him to Berlin. And hardly had her pride and joy sat down in the train, then he leaned back in a corner, fell asleep, had a crazy dream, and let himself be robbed blind by a dirty, rotten lowlife. And he's not supposed to cry? What was he supposed to do now? Get off the train in Berlin and say to Grandma, "Well, here I am. And guess what, you're not getting your money. But can I have some dough for my ticket back to New Town? Otherwise I'll have to walk . . ."?

Oh, this was just wonderful! Mom had saved all that money for nothing. And Grandma wasn't going to get a single penny of it. No way could he stay in Berlin. And he couldn't go home either. All because of that jerk who handed out chocolate to kids, pretended he was asleep, and then robbed them! Insanity! What kind of world was this?!

Emil's tears kept wanting to flow, but he choked them back and had a look around. If he pulled the emergency brake, the train would immediately come to a standstill. Then a conductor would come. And then another. And yet another. And they would all ask him, "What's going on?"

"I've been robbed," he would say.

And they'd say, "Next time you'll have to be more careful. Get back on the train. What's your name? Where do you live? Pulling that emergency brake will cost you a hundred marks. You'll get the bill in the mail."

In the express trains you could at least walk from car

to car, from one end of the train to the other, all the way to the conductor's compartment, and report the theft. But here! In a slow train like this! You had to wait until the next station, and then the man in the bowler would be miles away. Emil didn't even know at which station the guy had gotten out. What time was it anyway? When would they be in Berlin? Large buildings and mansions with colorful lawns wandered by the train windows, followed by more dirty red brick chimneys. This was probably Berlin already. He would have to find the conductor at the next station and tell him everything. And the conductor would immediately report it to the police!

Oh, brother! Now he'd have the police to deal with, too. Naturally, Officer Jeschke would have to say something and make a report, "I don't know, but I don't like the looks of that New Town schoolboy Emil Tabletoe. First he paints all over our venerable monuments. Then he lets himself get robbed of a hundred and forty marks. Maybe the money wasn't even stolen? Defacers of statues are likely to be liars, too. I've seen it before. Maybe he buried the money in the forest or hid it and plans to go to America with it? There's no sense in looking for the thief. The thief is Emil Tabletoe himself. I beg you, Your Honor, have him arrested."

This was terrible. He couldn't even tell the police!

He pulled his suitcase down from the luggage rack, put on his cap, stuck the pin back in his lapel, and got ready. He had no idea what he was going to do. But he couldn't stand to spend another five minutes in that compartment. That was certain.

In the meantime, the train had started slowing down. Emil saw a great number of gleaming rails outside. Then platforms slowly moving by. A couple of porters ran alongside the cars, hoping to earn a few marks.

The train stopped!

Emil looked out the window and saw, way up over the tracks, a sign: ZOO STATION. The doors flew open. People clambered out of the cars. Others were waiting and smiling out on the platform, their arms open wide.

Emil leaned far out the window, looking for the engineer. There, at some distance and in the middle of the crowd, he caught sight of a black bowler. Maybe it was the thief? Maybe he hadn't gotten off the train after robbing Emil, but simply went into another car?

Minutes later, Emil was standing on the platform. He put down his suitcase, went back inside the train because he'd left the flowers up on the luggage rack, returned to the platform, grabbed his suitcase, hoisted it up, and ran as fast as he could toward the exit.

Where had the bowler hat gone? The boy stumbled over people's legs, jabbed someone with the suitcase, but kept running. The crowd got more and more packed and impenetrable.

Over there! There was the bowler! But wait, there was another one over there! Emil could hardly carry the suitcase anymore. He really would've liked to set it down somewhere and leave it. But then his suitcase would get stolen, too!

Finally he pushed his way through to where the bowler hats were.

That could be him! Was it?

No.

There was the other one.

Not him either. Too short.

Emil slipped through the crowd like an Indian.

There! There!

That was him. Thank God! It was Groundsnow. He was just going through the gate and seemed to be in a hurry.

"Just wait, you slimeball!" Emil snarled. "We'll get you yet!" Then he gave the attendant his ticket, took his suitcase in the other hard, jammed the bouquet of flowers under his right arm, and followed the man down the steps.

This was it.

CHAPTER SIX

THE #177 STREETCAR

HE WOULD HAVE LIKED NOTHING MORE THAN TO RUN AFTER the guy, plant himself in front of him, and shout, "Give me my money back!" But the man didn't exactly look like the type to answer, "Why certainly, my boy. Here you are. I promise never to do it again." The problem wasn't so simple. The important thing now was to keep an eye on him.

Emil hid behind a big, broad-backed woman walking in front of him, and peered out on either side of her to make sure the man was still there and hadn't suddenly taken off on a long-distance run. The man, meanwhile, had made his way to the station's main entrance. He stood there, looking around and scanning the jostling crowd behind him as if he were searching for someone. Emil squeezed in behind the big lady as they got closer and closer to the man. What would happen now? In a minute he'd be walking past him, and then there'd be no point in hiding anymore. Maybe the lady would help him? But why should she believe him? And the thief would say, "Pardon me, ma'am, but do you think I look like someone who needs to steal from children?" Then everyone would look at Emil and say, "Some nerve! To badmouth a grown man like that! Young people today have no manners!" Emil's teeth were already chattering.

Luckily the man turned his head in the other direction and stepped out onto the sidewalk. The boy jumped behind the door in a flash, put down his suitcase, and peered through the latticed pane. Oh man, did his arm ever hurt!

The thief walked slowly across the street, looked back one more time, and kept walking, clearly reassured. Then a streetcar with the number 177 on it came rolling in from the left and stopped. The man thought for a moment then got into the front car and took a window seat.

Emil picked up his suitcase again and ran, ducking, back around the door and into the hall, found another door, ran into the street, and just as the streetcar was starting to move, he reached the trailer car. He threw his suitcase aboard, climbed up after it, shoved it into a corner, stood in front of it, and let out a deep breath. He made it!

But what would happen now? If the guy jumped off while the streetcar was moving, then the money was gone for good. There was no way Emil was going to jump off a moving streetcar with the suitcase. It was too dangerous.

All those cars! They rushed past the streetcar, their horns honking, beeping, red directionals sticking out left and right. They turned the corner, and other cars took their place. What a racket! And all the people on the sidewalks! Streetcars, horse-drawn carriages, double-decker buses on all sides! Newspaper vendors on every corner. Incredible window displays with flowers, fruits, books, gold watches, dresses, silk lingerie. And tall, tall buildings.

So this was Berlin.

Emil would have liked to observe it all at his own pace. But he didn't have time. In the front car was sitting a man who had Emil's money and who at any moment could get off and disappear in the crowd. Then it would all be over. Back out there, between the cars and people and buses, it would be impossible to find anybody. Emil stuck his head out. What if the guy had already taken off? Then he was riding the streetcar all by himself, without a clue where he was going or why. Meanwhile Grandma was waiting at the flower shop in Frederick Street Station, unaware that her grandson was cruising through Berlin on the 177, and was in a lot trouble. It was enough to drive you mad!

The streetcar made its first stop. Emil kept his eye peeled on the front car. But no one got off. Only a lot of new passengers pushed their way on. Past Emil, too. A man complained because Emil was sticking his head out the door and was in the way.

"Can't you see people are trying to get up the steps?" he growled.

The conductor, who was inside the streetcar selling tickets, pulled on a cord. A bell rang, and the streetcar took off again. Emil repositioned himself in his corner, got pushed back, got his feet stepped on, and with a shock he realized, "I don't have any money! If the conductor comes back here, I'll have to buy a ticket. And if I can't, he'll kick me off. And then I might as well dive off a cliff!"

He looked at the people standing around him. Maybe he could tug on one of their coats and ask, "Could you please lend me money for a ticket?" But their faces were so serious! One of them was reading a newspaper. Two others were talking about a bank robbery. "They actually dug a tunnel," said the one. "They went in and cleared out all the safe deposit boxes. Apparently the damages run to several million marks."

"But it will be enormously difficult to determine what was really in that vault," said the other man, "since the people who rent the safe-deposit boxes were under no obligation to tell the bank what they had in their boxes."

"Yeah, someone will probably claim he had a hundred thousand marks worth of diamonds, when actually it was just a stack of worthless banknotes or a dozen silver-plated spoons," added the first man. They both chuckled.

"That's exactly what will happen to me," thought Emil sadly. "I'll explain how Mr. Groundsnow stole a hundred and forty marks from me, and no one will believe me. Then the thief will say I'm being a smart-aleck, and that it was only three marks fifty. What a mess!"

The conductor kept getting closer to the door. Now he was standing in the doorway, shouting, "Who still doesn't have a ticket?"

He tore off large, white pieces of paper and perforated them with a hole-punch. The people on the running board gave him money and got tickets in return.

"So, what about you?" he asked the boy.

"I lost my money, sir," replied Emil. No one would have believed him if he said he'd been robbed.

"Lost your money, eh? I've heard that one. Where are you going?"

"I . . . I don't know yet," Emil stuttered.

"Well, then why don't you get off at the next stop and figure out where you want to go."

"I'm sorry, I can't, sir. I need to stay here. Please."

"When I tell you to get off, you have to get off. Got it?"

"Oh, give the boy a ticket!" said the man who had been reading the newspaper. He gave money to the conductor. And the conductor gave Emil a ticket and said to the man, "Do you have any idea how many kids ride the streetcar every day and claim they forgot their money? Afterwards they just laugh at us."

"This one here won't laugh at us."

The conductor returned to the inside of the car.

"Thank you so much, sir!" said Emil.

"Don't mention it. You're welcome." said the man, turning back to his newspaper.

Then the streetcar stopped again. Emil leaned out to see if the man in the bowler was getting off. But he saw nothing.

"May I please have your address?" Emil asked the man.

"What for?"

"So I can return the money to you as soon as I have some again. I'll be staying in Berlin for a week, so I can stop by your place one day. My name is Tabletoe. Emil Tabletoe from New Town."

"No," said the man, "just consider the ticket a gift. Do you need any more?"

"Certainly not!" Emil insisted. "I wouldn't accept it!"

"As you like," said the man and returned to his newspaper.

The streetcar went on. And stopped. Then kept going. Emil read the name of the beautiful, wide street. Emperor Avenue was its name. He had no idea where he was going to get out. There was a thief in the other car. And maybe other thieves were sitting or standing in the streetcar. No one paid him any attention. A stranger had just given him a ticket. But now he had turned back to his newspaper.

The city was so large. And Emil was so small. And not a soul cared why he had no money or that he didn't know where he was going. Four million people lived in Berlin, and not one of them was interested in Emil Tabletoe. No one was interested in anyone else's problems. Everyone had his or her own troubles and joys to deal with. And when people said, "Oh, I'm so sorry," usually what they meant was, "Don't bother me!"

What would happen? Emil swallowed hard. And he felt very, very alone.

CHAPTER SEVEN

AN UPROAR ON
SCHUMANN STREET

WHILE EMIL WAS STANDING IN THE #177 STREETCAR, RIDING down Emperor Avenue without a clue where he would end up, Grandma and Pony the Hat, his cousin, were waiting for him at Frederick Street Station. They stood in front of the flower shop, right where they said they would be, and kept looking at the clock. A lot of people walked past, with suitcases and trunks and boxes and briefcases and bouquets of flowers. But Emil was nowhere to be seen.

"He's probably gotten a lot bigger, huh?" said Pony the Hat, pushing her little nickel-plated bicycle back and forth. She actually wasn't supposed to take it, but she whined for so long that Grandma finally said, "Oh go on, bring it along, you silly goose!" Now the silly goose was in a good mood and couldn't wait to see the look of admiration on Emil's face. "He'll think it's the best bike ever," she said, and she couldn't have been more sure of herself.

Grandma was getting nervous. "I just wish I knew what was happening. It's already twenty past six. That train should have been here by now."

She hemmed and hawed a few more minutes. Then she sent the little girl off to find out what happened.

Naturally, Pony the Hat took her bicycle with her. "Excuse me, Mr. Ticket Inspector, could you please tell me why the train from New Town is so late?" she asked the man with the hole-punch who was standing at the gate, making sure that everyone who wanted to go through had a ticket.

"New Town? New Town?" He thought for a moment. "Ah yes, 6:17. That train already got in."

"Oh, that's really too bad, because we've been waiting over there by the flower stand for my cousin Emil."

"Glad to hear it. Glad to hear it," said the man.

"Why does that make you so glad, Mr. Ticket Inspector?" Pony wanted to know and gave the bell on her bike a few rings.

But the man just turned his back on the girl without answering her.

"You sure are weird!" Pony said. "Have a nice day!"

A few people laughed. The ticket inspector bit his lip in irritation. And Pony the Hat trotted back to the flower stand.

"The train already arrived, Grandma."

"What on earth can have happened?" The elderly woman wondered aloud. "If he didn't make it on the train in the first place, his mother would have let us know.

Maybe he got off at the wrong station? But we gave him such detailed instructions!"

"I can't make heads or tails of it," Pony declared, just like a grown-up. "I'm sure he got off at the wrong station. Sometimes boys can be really dumb. I bet that's what happened! Just wait, you'll see!"

And since they did not know what else to do, they started waiting again. Five minutes.

Another five minutes.

"This is getting pointless," said Pony to her grandmother. "We can stand here until we turn blue in the face. Maybe there's another flower stand somewhere?"

"Go look and find out. But don't be long!"

The Hat took her bike again and scoured the train station.

Far and wide there were no other flower stands. Then she quickly interrogated two train station employees before she returned, very proud of herself.

"Well," she began, "there are no other flower stands. Would be a little weird if there were. What else did I want to say? Oh, right, the next train from New Town gets here at eight thirty-three. Just a little after half past eight. So we should go on back home. And then at eight on the dot I'll ride my bike back over here. If he's not here by then, then he's getting a nasty old letter from me!"

"Watch your tongue, Pony!"

"I mean, he'll be getting a letter that's not very nice!"

Grandma made a worried face and shook her head.

"I just don't like the looks of it. I just don't like the looks of it," she said. When she was upset, she always said everything twice.

They walked slowly back home. On the way, as they were crossing the Meadowbank Bridge, Pony the Hat asked, "Grandma, do you want to ride on the handlebars?"

"Shut your mouth!"

"Why? You're not any heavier than Arthur Zickler. And he rides on the handlebars all the time."

"If your father sees that happen, he'll take that bike away from you for good!"

"Aww, I can't tell you people anything," Pony grumbled.

When they arrived home—15 Schumann Street—Pony's parents—the Heimbolds—were in an uproar. Everyone wanted to know where Emil was, and no one could say.

Pony's father suggested they call and tell Emil's mother.

"Absolutely not!" exclaimed his wife, Pony's mother. "She'll die of shock! Let's just go to the station again at eight o'clock. Maybe he'll be on the next train."

"Oh, I hope so!" moaned Grandma. "But I really must say, I don't like the looks of this. I just don't like the looks of it!"

"I just don't like the looks of it," said Pony the Hat and shook her little head back and forth.

CHAPTER EIGHT

THE BOY WITH THE BICYCLE HORN TURNS UP

AT THE CORNER OF EMPEROR AVENUE AND TRAUTENAU Street, the man in the bowler hat left the streetcar. Emil saw him, picked up his suitcase and bouquet of flowers, told the man reading the newspaper, "Once again, thank you so much, sir!" and stepped down out of the car.

The thief walked around the front of the streetcar, crossed the tracks, and maneuvered toward the other side of the street. Then the streetcar drove off, and Emil could see the man standing there on the sidewalk, hesitating, then walking up the steps of an outdoor café.

Once again he would have to be on his guard. Like a detective on the lookout for fleas, Emil shrewdly oriented himself. He saw a newspaper kiosk and darted behind it. His hiding place, between the kiosk and an advertising pillar, was excellent. The boy put down his baggage, took off his cap, and peered out.

The man had taken a seat on the patio, right next to the railing. He was smoking a cigarette and seemed quite pleased with himself. Emil was disgusted that a thief could be happy at all, when the one he'd robbed had to go around sad and demoralized.

What sense did it make, ultimately, for him to hide behind a newspaper kiosk as if he were the thief and not the other guy? So now that he knew the man was sitting in Café Josty on Emperor Avenue, drinking a pint of beer and smoking cigarettes—what was the point? If the guy were to get up now, the chase could continue. But if he decided to stay there, Emil could go on standing behind the newspaper kiosk until he'd grown himself a long, gray beard. All he needed now was for a patrolman to turn up and say, "Son, you look like you're up to something. Come on with me and don't make a scene. Otherwise I'll have to cuff you."

Suddenly Emil heard a loud honk right behind him. He jumped to the side, spun around, and saw a boy standing there, laughing at him. "Hey man, settle down!" said the boy.

"Who was that honking behind me?" asked Emil.

"That was me, of course. So I guess you're not from Wilmersdorf? If you were, you'd know I always carry a horn around with me. I'm like a circus freak in these parts; everyone knows me."

"I'm from New Town. I just got here."

"From New Town, huh? So is that why you're wearing that dumb suit?"

"Take that back! If you don't, I'll knock you out!"

"Whoa!" the other boy said cheerfully. "Are you crazy? This weather is way too nice for boxing. But sure, I'll fight you!"

"I'll have to take a rain check," said Emil. "No time right now." And he glanced back at the café, to see if Groundsnow was still sitting there.

"Looks to me like you have lots of time! Standing there with your suitcase and cauliflowers behind a newspaper stand, playing hide-and-seek all by your lonesome! You must have a good twenty, thirty yards of time to spare."

"No," said Emil, "I'm keeping tabs on a thief."

"What? A thief?" said the other boy. "Who did he rob?"

"Me!" said Emil and was even proud of the fact. "In the train. While I was sleeping. A hundred and forty marks. I was supposed to give it to my grandmother here in Berlin. Then he slipped into another compartment and got out at Zoo Station. Of course, I was right on his heels. In the streetcar, too. Now he's sitting over there in the café, the one in the bowler, living it up."

"Dude, that's so awesome!" shouted the other boy. "It's like in the movies! What are you going to do?"

"I have no idea. I guess for now I'll just keep following him."

"Tell the patrolman over there. He'll bust him for sure."

"I'd rather not. I pulled some stuff back in New Town. They may have it in for me. And if I—"

"I hear you."

"And my grandmother is waiting for me at Frederick Street Station."

The boy with the horn thought for a while. Then he said, "Listen, this thing with the robber is cool. It's awesome, actually! So unless you have a problem with it, I'd like to help out."

"Wow, that would be great of you!"

"It's no big deal. Of course I'm game. By the way, my name is Gus."

"And I'm Emil."

They shook hands, and it was like they were already good friends.

"Let's go," said Gus. "If we just stand around here, that rat will slip through our fingers. You have any dough left?"

"Not a cent."

Gus honked a little, to get his thoughts going. But it didn't help.

"How about if you got a few more friends to come?" suggested Emil.

"Man, that's a great idea!" shouted Gus excitedly. "I'll do it! All I have to do is whistle and honk through the courtyards and we'll have a full house."

"Do it!" said Emil. "But come back soon. Otherwise that guy will take off. And I'll have no choice but to trail him. Then when you get here I'll be miles away."

"No worries! I'll be quick! You can depend on it. Anyway, Mousebait over there is eating Eggs Benedict and stuff like that. He's in no hurry to leave. So, see you later, Emil! Man, I am so psyched. This is going to be awesome!" And with that he zoomed off. Emil was incredibly relieved. Bad luck is bad luck, any way you cut it. But having a few pals to help you out always makes things better.

He kept his eyes peeled on the thief, who was enjoying his meal—paid for, no doubt, with Mom's savings. He was afraid of only one thing: The scumbag would stand up and run off again. Then he could just forget about Gus and the horn and everything.

But Mr. Groundsnow did him a favor and stayed put. Of course, if he'd had any clue about the conspiracy that was drawing around him like a sack, he would have ordered the first airplane out of there, at least. His situation was starting to get dicey . . .

Ten minutes later Emil heard the horn again. He turned around and saw at least two dozen boys, Gus in the lead, marching up Trautenau Street.

"That's all of us! So, what do you say?" asked Gus, beaming.

"Man, I'm really moved," said Emil. He was so happy he poked Gus in the ribs.

"So, gentlemen! This here is Emil from New Town. I've already told you what the deal is. The dog who stole his money is sitting at that cafe. The guy on the right, with

the black melon on his dome. If we let our friend over there get away, we'll all be wearing permanent dunce caps after tomorrow. You get me?"

"We'll get him, Gus!" said a boy with horn-rimmed glasses.

"This is the Professor," explained Gus. And Emil shook his hand.

Then, one by one, the whole gang was introduced.

"So," said the Professor, "let's get this show on the road! But first, your money!"

Everybody gave what he had. The coins dropped into Emil's cap. Someone even put in a whole mark. That was Tuesday, a very small boy who jumped excitedly from one leg to the other and who got to count the money. "Our capital," he informed his anxious listeners, "comes to five marks and seventy cents. The best thing would be to divide the money three ways. Just in case we have to split up."

"Excellent," said the Professor. He and Emil each got two marks. Gus got one mark seventy.

"Thanks so much," said Emil. "After we catch him, I'll give you the money back. So what do we do now? I'd really like to stash my suitcase and these flowers some-where. They'll be in the way when the chase gets going."

"Man, just give your stuff to me," said Gus. "I'll take it over to Café Josty, leave it at the counter, and sniff out our friend the thief while I'm at it."

"But watch your step," advised the Professor. "That jerk doesn't need to catch on that detectives are on his trail. It'll make following him that much harder."

"You think I'm dense or something?" Gus growled and took off.

"That guy'll make a great mugshot," he said when he returned. "And your things are in good hands. We can pick them up whenever."

"This would be a good time," suggested Emil, "to plan our strategy. But not here. We're too visible."

"Let's go to Nikolsburg Square," suggested the Professor. "Two of us will stay here at the newspaper kiosk and make sure the guy doesn't slip away. Five or six will act as messengers and send word when the time comes. Then we'll rush back."

"I'm your man!" Gus shouted and began organizing the messengers. "I'll stay here with the guards," he said to Emil. "Don't worry! We won't let him out of our sight. But hurry up. It's already a little past seven. So, get going!"

He assigned the messengers to their places. And the others, with Emil and the Professor in the lead, moved to Nikolsburg Square.

CHAPTER NINE

THE DETECTIVES HOLD COUNCIL

THEY SAT DOWN ON TWO WHITE BENCHES IN THE GRASSY area, and on the low iron railing surrounding it, and furrowed their brows. The boy known as the Professor seemed to have been waiting for this day. He kept taking off his horn-rimmed glasses, just like his father the judge would do, and fiddling with them as he devised his plan.

"There is a distinct possibility," he began, "that we will have to separate later on for practical reasons. That's why we need a telephone operator. Who here has a phone?"

Twelve boys raised their hands.

"And of those who have telephones, who has the most levelheaded parents?"

"Probably me!" shouted little Tuesday.

"Your phone number?"

"Bavaria 0579."

"Here's some paper and a pencil. Crumbagel, please prepare twenty strips of paper and write Tuesday's phone number on each one. But make sure it's legible! And make sure we each get one. The telephone operator will always know where the detectives are and what is going on. If any of you need information, then just call up little Tuesday and he'll give it you."

"But I won't be there," said little Tuesday.

"Yes, you will," replied the Professor. "As soon as we're finished with our council meeting here, you're going home and manning the telephone."

"Oh, but I'd rather be out here with you guys when that guy gets caught. Little kids can come in handy with things like that."

"You're going home and staying by the phone. It is an important job and a big responsibility."

"Oh all right, if you say so."

Crumbagel distributed the telephone numbers. And the boys all carefully put the strips of paper away in their pockets. A few particularly diligent ones learned the number by heart.

"We should have some backups, too," said Emil.

"Naturally. Anyone who isn't absolutely necessary for the chase will stay here at Nikolsburg Square. You'll take turns going home. Tell your parents you might be out late tonight. A few of you might even say you're spending the night at a friend's. This is so we'll have substitutes and reinforcements in case we don't catch him before tomorrow morning. Gus, Crumbagel, Arnold Middleday, his brother, and I will all call our parents and tell them that we'll be home late. . . . And Truegut will go with Tuesday as a go-between and run to Nikolsburg Square when we need someone. So that gives us detectives, reinforcements, a telephone operator, and a go-between. All the basic divisions are taken care of.

"We'll need something to eat," Emil pointed out. "Maybe a few of you could run home and get some sandwiches."

"Who lives closest to here?" asked the Professor. "Middleday, Gerold, Freddie the Great, Brunot, Zerlett! Get moving—and bring back some chow with you!"

The five boys jumped up and raced off.

"You knuckleheads! You keep going on about food and telephones and sleeping in shifts. But you haven't given a thought to how you're going to catch the thief. You're a bunch of . . . a bunch of schoolteachers!" growled Truegut. He couldn't think of anything worse to call them.

"Do you have a machine for reading fingerprints?" asked Petzold. "If he was really sly, he might have had gloves on. And then you won't have any evidence." Petzold had already seen twenty-two detective films, and anyone could see they hadn't done him much good.

"Give me a break!" said Truegut, rolling his eyes. "We'll just wait for the right moment, then steal back the money he stole from Emil!"

"No way!" said the Professor. "If we steal the money from him, then were just as much thieves as he is!"

"Oh, right!" retorted Truegut. "If someone steals something from me, and I steal it back, that doesn't make me a thief!"

"Yes it does," insisted the Professor.

"You don't know what you're talking about," grumbled Truegut.

"I think the Professor is right," Emil broke in. "If I take something away from someone in secret, then I'm a thief. It doesn't matter if it belongs to him or if he stole it from me first."

"Exactly," said the Professor. "Do me a favor and lay off the clever speeches. They're not helpful. So, it looks like we're ready for the hunt. We still can't know how we'll bag our quarry. But we'll figure something out. In any case, he has to give up the money voluntarily. To steal it would be idiotic."

"I don't understand," said little Tuesday. "If it already belongs to me, then I can't steal it. If it belongs to me, then it's mine, even if it's in someone else's pocket!"

"Those are finer points that are hard to understand," the Professor lectured. "Morally you may be right. But the court will condemn you anyway. Many adults don't understand this either. But that's how it is."

"Have it your way," Truegut said and shrugged.

"And make sure you're sneaky! Are you good at sneaking?" asked Petzold. "If you're not, he'll turn around and see you. Okay, so long!"

"Yeah, it's important to know how to sneak," little Tuesday confirmed. "That's why I was thinking you could use me. Boy, can I ever sneak! I'd make a really great police dog. I can even bark."

"Try sneaking in Berlin and see if no one notices you!" Emil exclaimed. "If you really want everyone to notice you, all you need to do is start sneaking around."

"But you'll need a pistol!" Petzold advised. He just wouldn't let up with the suggestions.

"Yeah, a pistol!" shouted two or three others.

"No," said the Professor.

"The thief has one for sure," Truegut wanted to bet.

"The situation is dangerous," Emil confirmed. "So anyone who's scared should go home and go to bed."

"Are you calling me a coward?" Truegut asked and stepped into the middle like a boxer entering the ring.

"Order!" shouted the Professor. "You can clobber each other tomorrow! What is this? You're acting like . . . like children!"

"Well, we are children," said little Tuesday. And everyone laughed.

"Actually, I should write a note to my grandmother. My relatives have no idea where I am. They might even go to the police. Could someone deliver a letter for me while we're going after that guy? They live at 15 Schumann Street. I'd really appreciate it."

"I'll do it," said a boy named Bleuer. "But write fast! So I can make it there before they lock the building door.

I'll take the subway to Oranienburg Gate. Who'll spot me the cash?"

The Professor gave him money for the fare. Twenty cents, there and back. Emil borrowed a pencil and sheet of paper, and wrote:

> Dear Grandma,
>
> I'm sure you're all wondering where I am. I'm in Berlin. But unfortunately I can't come just yet, because there's something important I have to take care of first. Don't ask what it is. And don't worry about me. I'll come when everything's been settled. I can hardly wait! The boy who's giving you this letter is a friend of mine and knows where I am. But he can't tell you. It's an official secret. Give my love to Uncle Robert, Aunt Martha, and Pony the Hat.
>
> Love, Emil
>
> P.S. Mom sends her love, too. And I have some flowers, which I'll give you as soon as I can.

Emil wrote the address on the other side, folded the sheet, and said, "Just make sure you don't tell my relatives where I am or that the money's out the window. If you do, I'm done for."

"No problem, Emil!" said Bleuer. "Give me the

telegram. When I get back, I'll call up Tuesday to find out what's happening. Then I'll report to the backup team." Then he raced away.

In the meantime the five boys had returned, bringing bags full of sandwiches with them. Gerold produced a whole sausage. His mother gave it to him. Or so he claimed.

The five boys had told their parents they might be out for a few more hours.

Emil distributed the sandwiches, and everyone stuck one in his pocket for reserve. Emil himself took responsibility for the sausage.

Then five other boys ran home to ask if they could stay out late. Two of them didn't come back. Their parents probably wouldn't let them.

The Professor gave them the code word. So that when anyone came or called on the phone, the others would know right away if he was one of them. The code word was "Emil!" That was easy to remember.

At that point little Tuesday told the detectives to break a leg, and he and Truegut, the grumpy go-between, took off. The Professor shouted after him, asking him if he would call his, the Professor's, house and tell his father that he had an urgent matter to attend to. "That will reassure him, and he'll be fine with it," he added.

"Unbelievable," said Emil. "Berlin parents are so cool!"

"Don't kid yourself. They're not all so wonderful," said Crumbagel, scratching behind his ear.

"No, it's true. On average they're all right," said the Professor. "It's also very smart of them. That way they don't get lied to. I promised my father that I would never do anything immoral or dangerous. And as long as I keep my word, I can do whatever I want. My father's a good guy."

"That's great!" Emil said again. "But hey, what if things do get dangerous tonight?"

"Then the permission is cancelled," said the Professor and shrugged. "He told me I should always ask myself if I would act any differently if he were there with me. And I know I wouldn't tonight. Anyway, let's get this show on the road."

He planted himself in front of the group of boys and exclaimed, "The detectives expect you to do your job. We've set up the telephone hub. I'm leaving you my money. There's a mark and fifty cents left. Here, Gerold, take it and count it. We have provisions. We have money. Everyone knows the phone number. One more thing: If anyone needs to go home, then beat it! But we need at least five people to stay. Gerold, you'll be responsible for that. Show us that you're real boys! In the meantime, we'll be doing our best. If we need replacements, little Tuesday will send Truegut to you. Any questions? Have I made myself clear? Code word Emil!"

"Code word Emil!" the boys all shouted so loudly that Nikolsburg Square began to rumble and the people walking by all glared.

Emil was downright glad that he'd been robbed.

CHAPTER TEN

CHASING THE TAXI

SUDDENLY THREE MESSENGERS CAME RUSHING OUT OF Trautenau Street, waving their arms.

"Let's go!" shouted the Professor. And he, Emil, the Middleday brothers, and Crumbagel all sprinted to Emperor Avenue as if they were trying to break the world record for the hundred-yard dash. Then Gus signaled to them to slow down, and they took the last thirty feet before the newspaper stand at a walk, trying to be careful.

"Too late?" asked Emil, out of breath.

"Are you crazy, bud?" whispered Gus. "When I do a job, I do it right."

The thief was standing on the other side of the street in front of Café Josty, looking around like a tourist in Switzerland. Then he bought the evening newspaper from a newspaper vendor and began to read.

"If he comes over here and sees us, it'll be messy," said Crumbagel.

They stood behind the kiosk, stuck their heads out around the side, and trembled with excitement. The thief didn't notice them in the slightest. He was doggedly turning every page of the newspaper.

"I bet he's looking out the corner of his eye to see if anyone's on his trail," was the elder Middleday's assessment.

"Did he look over this way often?" asked the Professor.

"Not at all, bud! He kept chowing down like he hadn't eaten in three days."

"Hey, look!" exclaimed Emil.

The man in the bowler hat folded up his newspaper and eyed the people walking past him. Then out of the blue he waved down a vacant taxi driving by. The car stopped. The man got in. The car drove on.

But by then the boys were already sitting in another taxi, and Gus was telling the driver, "See that cab turning now onto Prague Place? You do? Then please follow it. But make sure he doesn't notice you."

The car sped up, crossed Emperor Avenue and followed the other taxi at a safe distance.

"What's going on?" asked the driver.

"Man, this guy up there pulled a fast one, and we're not letting him out of our sight," Gus explained. "But keep it to yourself, all right?"

"As you wish," replied the driver, then asked, "Do you even have money?"

"What do you think we are?" said the Professor reproachfully.

"Easy now," grumbled the man.

"IA 3733 is the license plate number," Emil announced.

"That's important," said the Professor and wrote down the number.

"Don't get too close to them!" warned Crumbagel.

"Don't worry about it," murmured the driver.

So they drove down Motz Street, past Victoria Louisa Square, and then down more of Motz Street. A few people stopped on the sidewalk, stared after the car, and had a laugh over the strange company in it.

"Duck!" whispered Gus. The boys threw themselves to the floor and lay there like a heap of cabbages and turnips.

"What is it?" asked the Professor.

"There's a red light at Luther Street, dude! We'll have to stop there, and the other car won't make it through either."

Both cars did stop and wait, one behind the other, until the light turned green and they continued through the intersection. But no one could tell that the second taxi was occupied. It looked empty. The boys were crouching down like pros. The driver turned around, saw the lot of them back there, and had to laugh. Once the taxi started moving, they carefully crept back up onto the seat.

"Hopefully it won't take much longer," said the Professor, eyeing the taxi meter. "This little ride has already cost us eighty cents."

But as it turned out the little ride was soon over. The first taxi stopped at Nollendorf Square, right in front of Hotel

Kreid. The second taxi stopped just in time and waited, outside the danger zone, for whatever would happen next.

The man in the bowler hat got out of his cab, paid, and disappeared into the hotel.

"Follow him, Gus!" said the Professor anxiously. "If that place has a back door, we'll lose him." Gus took off.

The other boys piled out. Emil paid. It cost one mark. The Professor quickly led his group into the entryway of a building that led past a cinema and into a large courtyard stretching out behind both the cinema and the Nollendorf Square Theater. He sent Crumbagel ahead to catch up with Gus.

"We'll be lucky if the guy stays in the hotel," Emil determined. "This courtyard would make a great headquarters."

"With all the modern conveniences," agreed the Professor. "Subway across the street, bushes for hiding, cafés for making phone calls. It doesn't get any better."

"Hopefully Gus will be on the ball," said Emil.

"You can depend on him," said Middleday Senior. "He's not as dumb as he looks."

"If only he would get here soon," said the Professor, sitting down on a chair that had been left out in the courtyard. He looked like Napoleon at the Battle of Leipzig.

Then Gus came back. "I think we got him," he said, rubbing his hands. "He parked right in the hotel. I saw the bellboy taking him up to his room. And they don't have a back door; I cased the joint from all sides. If he doesn't get out over the roof, we've got him trapped."

"Crumbagel's standing guard?" asked the Professor.

"Of course!"

Then Middleday Senior got some change, ran into a café and called up little Tuesday.

"Hello, Tuesday?"

"Yep, I'm here!" little Tuesday crowed on the other end of the line.

"Code word Emil! Middleday Senior here. The man in the bowler is staying at Hotel Kreid on Nollendorf Square. Our headquarters is in the courtyard of Cinema West, left entrance."

Little Tuesday wrote down all the details, repeated them back to him, and asked "Do you need any backups, Middleman?"

"Nope!"

"Has it been hard so far?"

"It's been okay. The guy took a cab, and we trailed him the whole time in another one, see, and then he got out here. He got a room and is up there now. Probably checking to see if the monsters are playing solitaire under his bed."

"What's the room number?"

"We don't know that yet. But we'll find out soon."

"Oh, I really wish I could be there! You know, after summer vacation is over and we have to write our first essays, I'm going to write about this."

"Did anyone else call yet?"

"No, nobody. It stinks."

"Well, so long, little Tuesday."

"Good luck, gentlemen! Oh, I just remembered: Code word Emil!"

"Code word Emil!" replied Middleday and reported back at the courtyard of Cinema West. It was already eight o'clock. The Professor left to check on the look-outs.

"Well, we're definitely not catching him tonight," said an irritated Gus.

"We're still better off if he goes to sleep right away," Emil pointed out, "than if he races around all night in a taxi, going out to eat, or dancing, or to the theater, or all three. If he does that, we'll have to apply for foreign aid just to keep up with him."

The Professor came back, sent the two Middleday brothers off to Nollendorf Square as go-betweens, and seemed lost in thought. "We'll have to figure out a better way to keep tabs on him," he said. "Put your heads together and think."

So they sat there for a while and brooded.

A bell rang in the courtyard, and in rolled a little nickel-plated bicycle. A little girl was sitting on it, and behind her, standing on the wheel, was their friend Bleuer. The two shouted, "Yippee!"

Emil jumped up, helped them off the bike, excitedly shook the little girl's hand, and said to the others, "This is my cousin, Pony the Hat."

The Professor politely offered the Hat his chair, and she sat down.

"Emil, you shark!" she said. "Comes to Berlin and starts shooting a movie! We were about to go back to Frederick Street Station for the New Town train, when your pal Bleuer came with your letter. Nice guy, by the way. Good work!"

Bleuer blushed and puffed out his chest.

"Anyway," Pony continued, "Mom and Dad and Grandma are sitting at home knocking themselves out, trying to figure out what happened to you. We didn't tell them anything, of course. I just took Bleuer out in front of the house and showed him what's what. I have to go right back home, though. If I don't, they'll call the National Guard out. Two kids missing in one day, their nerves couldn't handle it."

"Here, we saved the ten cents for the ride back," said Bleuer proudly. The Professor put the money away.

"Were they mad?" asked Emil.

"Not in the least," said the Hat. "Grandma kept galopping around the room, saying, 'My grandson Emil went to pay a visit to the president!' until Mom and Dad calmed her down. But do you think you'll get that guy tomorrow? Who's your Sherlock Holmes?"

"Here," said Emil. "This is the Professor."

"Pleased to meet you, Professor," said the Hat. "Finally—a real detective!"

The Professor laughed nervously and stuttered a few incomprehensible words.

"Well then," said Pony, "here's my allowance, twenty-five cents. Buy yourselves a few cigars."

Emil took the money. Pony sat on the chair like a beauty queen, and the boys stood around her like the judges.

"And now I'll make myself scarce," said Pony the Hat. "I'll be back tomorrow morning. Where will you all sleep? God, wouldn't I love to stick around and make coffee for you. But what can I do? A good girl's place is in her cage. Well, so long fellas! Good night, Emil!"

She gave Emil a jab on the shoulder, jumped up on her bike, cheerfully rang the bell, and rode off.

The boys stood for a long while without saying a word.

Then the Professor opened his mouth and said,

"Damn!"

And the others completely agreed.

CHAPTER ELEVEN

A SPY SNEAKS INTO THE HOTEL

TIME PASSED SLOWLY.

Emil went to see the three look-outs and offered to relieve one of them. But Crumbagel and both of the Middledays said they were staying. Then Emil went all the way up to Hotel Kreid itself to check out the situation. He came back to the courtyard all excited.

"I have a feeling," he said, "that something's going to give. We can't just leave the hotel for a whole night without a spy in there, even with Crumbagel at the corner of Kleist Street. All he has to do is look in the other direction and Groundsnow can vanish into thin air."

"That's easier said than done," said Gus. "We can't just go to the porter and say, 'Listen up, Boss, we're hanging out on these steps here whether you like it or not.' And you aren't stepping one foot in the hotel. The minute that jerk looks out his door and sees you, the game is up."

"That's not what I mean," answered Emil.

"Then what do you mean?" asked the Professor.

"In the hotel, there's this kid. He's in charge of the elevator and stuff like that. Let's say one of us goes and tells him what's up. Well, he's got to know the hotel like the back of his hand. He could help us for sure."

"Very good," said the Professor. "Excellent, in fact!" He had a funny habit. It was always like he was giving grades to the others. That's actually why they called him the Professor.

"Man! Another idea like that and we'll give you an honorary degree. Emil's so smart, you'd think he was from Berlin!" cried Gus.

"Hey, you're not the only ones who are smart!" Emil was sore. His New Town pride was wounded. "Anyway, we still have to box."

"What for?" asked the Professor.

"Oh, he made fun of my suit."

"Then the boxing match will take place tomorrow," the Professor decided. "Tomorrow or not at all."

"Hey, your suit really isn't so dumb. I'm used to it now," said Gus goodheartedly. "But we can still box if you want. I probably should let you know, though, that I'm the neighborhood champ. You better watch out!"

"And I'm the best in practically every weight class in my school," claimed Emil.

"You tough guys are driving me nuts!" exclaimed the Professor. "I was planning on going over to the hotel myself. But I see I can't leave you two alone for a minute. You'll be pounding each other in no time."

"Then I'll go!" suggested Gus.

"Exactly!" agreed the Professor. "Then you go. And you talk with the bellboy. But watch your step! Maybe you can figure something out. Find out what room the guy is staying in. Be back in an hour and give us a report."

Gus took off.

The Professor and Emil walked out in front of the building and told each other about their teachers. Then the Professor explained all the local and international license plates on the cars driving past until Emil started to recognize them on his own. Then they split a sandwich.

It was already getting dark. Everywhere neon signs were flickering up. The elevated train thundered past. The subway rumbled. The streetcars and buses, cars and bicycles were putting on a crazy concert. In Café Woerz, dance music was playing. The movie houses on Nollendorf Square were starting their last show of the evening, and people were crowding to get in.

"A huge tree like that one by the station," said Emil, "seems pretty weird here, don't you think? It looks like it got lost." The boy was captivated and moved. He almost forgot why he was standing there and that he had lost the hundred and forty marks.

"Berlin is pretty amazing. It's like being at the movies. But I really don't know if I'd want to live here forever. In New Town we have our main square and our little main square and the square in front of the train station. And the playgrounds along the river and at Blackbird Park. That's it. But you know what, Professor? I think that's enough for me. To have all this hustle and bustle around you all the time, or all these thousands of streets and intersections? I'd always be getting lost. I don't know what I'd do if I didn't have you guys, if I was standing here by myself! It gives me goosebumps."

"You get used to it," said the Professor. "I probably couldn't handle living in New Town either, with its three squares and Blackbird Park."

"You get used to it," said Emil. "But Berlin is great. No doubt about it, Professor. Really great."

"Is your mom very strict?" the Berlin boy asked.

"Mom?" asked Emil. "Not at all. She lets me do anything I want. But I don't. You know what I mean?"

"No," said the Professor honestly, "I don't know what you mean."

"No? Well, it's like this. Does your family have a lot of money?"

"I don't know. We never really talk about it."

"I think when people don't talk about money at home, it means they have some."

The Professor considered this for a moment and said, "That could well be."

"You see, Mom and I, we talk about it a lot, but we really don't have any. She's constantly trying to make money, and it's still never enough. But whenever we go on a field trip at school, Mom gives me just as much as the other boys get. Sometimes even more."

"How can she do that?"

"I don't know. But she does. And I always bring her back half."

"Does she want you to?"

"No way! But I want to."

"Oh, I see," said the Professor, "so that's how it is in your family."

"Yep. That's how it is. And when she tells me I can go out to the fields with the kid who lives upstairs until nine at night, then I'm always back by seven. I can't stand to think of her sitting in the kitchen, eating supper alone. She still always tells me I should stay out with my friends. But when I tried doing it, it just wasn't fun anymore. Anyway, it really does make her happy that I come home early."

"Well, things are a lot different with my folks," said the Professor. "Whenever I actually make it home on time, they're sure to be at the theater or visiting friends. We do like each other. No question about it. We just don't practice it much."

"With us, liking each other is the one thing we can afford! That's why I'm no momma's boy. And if anyone says I am, I'll slam him up against the wall. It's really not hard to understand."

"I understand it."

The two boy stood for a while in the entryway without talking. Night fell. The stars glittered, and the moon squinted with its one eye over the elevated train tracks.

The Professor cleared his throat. Without looking at Emil, he asked him, "So I guess you and your mom really love each other, huh?"

"You bet we do," answered Emil.

CHAPTER TWELVE

A GREEN BELLBOY
SHOWS HIS COLORS

AROUND TEN O'CLOCK A DELEGATION OF BACKUPS SHOWED up in the courtyard with enough sandwiches to feed a hundred hungering peoples. They asked for further orders. The Professor was furious and told them they had no business coming, but should be waiting on Nikolsburg Square for Truegut, the go-between with the telephone hub.

"Don't be such a jerk!" said Petzold. "We were just wondering what was going on here."

"And anyway, we thought something happened to you, because Truegut never showed up," added Gerold, apologetically.

"How many are still at Nikolsburg Square?" asked Emil.

"Four. Maybe three," answered Freddie the Great.

"There might only be two left," said Gerold.

"Don't ask any more," exclaimed an enraged

Professor. "Next they'll tell us there's no one there at all!"

"Why are you yelling?" said Petzold. "And who the hell are you to tell me what to do?"

"I move that Petzold be dismissed immediately and forbidden from taking part in the chase," said the Professor and stomped his foot.

"I'm sorry you're arguing because of me," said Emil. "We should vote like they do in parliament. I move that Petzold simply be given a warning. Because we can't all just do whatever we like."

"Don't be so arrogant, you idiots. I'm going anyway, just so you know!" Then Petzold said something else that was extraordinarily rude and took off.

"He was the one who put us up to it. That's the only reason we came here," said Gerold. "Zerlett is still back at the reserve camp."

"Not another word about Petzold," the Professor ordered. His voice had gotten quiet again, and he was completely in control of himself. "He's history."

"And what will happen to us?" asked Freddie the Great.

"It's best if you wait until Gus comes back from the hotel and gives us a report," Emil suggested.

"Good idea," said the Professor. "Isn't that the bell-boy over there?"

"Yeah, that's him," Emil confirmed.

Standing in the entranceway was a boy wearing an entirely green uniform and a cap the same color on his head. He waved and slowly came toward them.

"Man, look at that cool uniform he has on!" said Gerold enviously.

"Do you have any news from our spy Gustav?" the Professor called out.

The boy was already pretty close to them. He nodded and said, "Yep."

"So what's the story?" Emil asked eagerly.

Suddenly a horn honked. And the boy in green jumped up and down in the entryway like a madman, laughing. "Man, Emil!" he shouted, "You are so dumb!"

It wasn't the boy at all; it was none other than Gus.

"Look, it's a leprechaun!" Emil pretended to make fun of him. And everyone had a good laugh until someone opened one of the windows overlooking the courtyard and shouted, "Pipe down out there!"

"Excellent!" said the Professor, "But let's keep it down, gentlemen. Gus, come over here and tell us everything."

"It's like in the movies, bud. Totally wild. Listen to this. So there I am sneaking into the hotel. I see the bellboy standing around and wave him over. He comes up to me, right, and I give him the scoop. From A to Z, more or less. I tell him about Emil. About us. And about the thief. And that the guy's staying in the hotel. And that we're busting a gut keeping watch over him so we can track down that money again tomorrow.

"'Great,' he says. 'I have an extra uniform. You can wear it and play the other bellboy.'

"'But what will the porter say? I'm sure he'll be mad,' I said to him.

"'Oh, the porter won't be mad. He'll be fine with it,' the bellboy said. 'He's my dad.'

"I have no idea what he said to his old man. But whatever it was, I got this uniform here, and they're letting me stay in an empty room for the staff, and I can even bring someone with me. So what do you all say to that?"

"What room is the thief staying in?" asked the Professor.

"Man, what is it with you? You're impossible to impress!" Gus grumbled, insulted. "Naturally I don't have to do anything. Just keep out of the way is all. The bellboy thought the thief checked into room 61, a single room, no shower, no nothing. So I go up to the third floor and start playing spy. Completely inconspicuous, of course. Hiding on the other side of the stairs and stuff. After a half hour or so the door to room 61 actually opens. And who should come marching out? None other than Ol' Pickpocket! He had to go use the—well, you know. I had a good look at him this afternoon, and it was him! Short, black moustache; ears so thin you could see the moon shining through them; and a face I wouldn't trade mine with for anything! As he was coming back from the—well, you know—I mosey up to him, stand my ground, and ask, 'Are you looking for something, sir? Anything I can help you with, sir?'

"'No,' he says, 'I don't need anything. Well, actually . . . Wait! Tell the porter to wake me up at eight. Room 61. And don't forget!'

"'Oh no, you can depend on me, sir!' I say, pinching my leg with excitement. 'I sure won't forget that, sir! The phone in room 61 will ring at eight o'clock sharp.' They wake people up by phone, you know. Then our thief just nodded, satisfied, and crept back into his lair."

"Excellent!" The Professor was more than satisfied, and the others were pretty happy about it, too. "We'll wait for him in front of the hotel after eight. Then the chase will continue. And then we'll catch him."

"He's a dead man," said Gerold.

"'Please omit flowers,'" said Gus. "Well, I gotta take off. I said I'd drop a letter in the mailbox for room 12. Fifty cent tip. This job pays pretty well! Somedays the bellboy makes ten marks in tips. He says. So, anyway, I'll be up around seven o'clock and make sure our scoundrel gets woken up on time. And then I'll make my way back down here."

"Man, Gus, I am so grateful to you," said Emil, almost like he was giving a speech. "Nothing more can happen now. Tomorrow we'll have him snared. And now we can all go home and go to bed. What do you say, Professor?"

"By all means. Let's all take off and get a good night's sleep. All those present will be back here tomorrow morning, at eight o'clock sharp. And if anyone can get hold of a little dough, please do. I'll call little Tuesday now. I'll ask him to have everyone who reports tomorrow show up here as reinforcements. We may have to organize a blockade. You never know."

"I'll go with Gus and sleep in the hotel," said Emil.

"Let's go, bud! You'll love it. It's a big ol' flea trap!"

"I'll make that phone call first," said the Professor, "then I'll go home, too, and relieve Zerlett on the way. Otherwise he'll still be sitting at Nikolsburg Square tomorrow morning, waiting for commands. Okay, have I made myself clear?"

"Yessirree, Commissioner!" Gus laughed.

"Tomorrow morning, eight o'clock sharp, here in the courtyard," said Gerold.

"Oh, and bring money," Freddie the Great remembered.

They said goodbye to each other, shaking each other's hands like little businessmen. Some of them marched off home. Gus and Emil went to the hotel. The Professor walked diagonally across Nollendorf Square in order to call little Tuesday from Café Hahnen.

An hour later they were all asleep, most of them in their own beds, two in staff quarters, on the fourth floor of Hotel Kreid.

And one next to the telephone, in Dad's armchair. That one was little Tuesday. He refused to leave his post. Truegut had gone home. But little Tuesday wouldn't budge from the phone. He curled up on the upholstered seat and slept and dreamed of four million telephone calls.

At midnight his parents got back from the theater. They were a little surprised to see their son in the armchair.

His mother picked him up and carried him off to bed. He flinched and murmured in his sleep, "Code word Emil!"

CHAPTER THIRTEEN

MR. GROUNDSNOW
GETS AN ESCORT

THE WINDOWS OF ROOM 61 FACED NOLLENDORF SQUARE. And as Mr. Groundsnow was combing his hair the next morning, he looked out and noticed the crowd of children hanging around down below. There were at least two dozen children playing kickball in front of the bushes across the street. Another division was posted on Kleist Street. Children were standing at the entrance to the subway.

"Must be on vacation," he growled, irritated, as he fastened his tie.

Meanwhile the Professor was running a party convention, ranting and raving at the delegates. "So here we are, burning the midnight oil, figuring out how to catch the guy, while you bunglers are out rousing the whole city! You think we need an audience? You think we're making a movie or something? If that guy slips away, it'll be your fault, you busybodies!"

The others stood there in a circle and listened patiently, but hardly seemed to be suffering any pangs of conscience. Maybe a few pinpricks. Gerold said, "Don't get worked up, Professor. We'll catch the robber either way."

"Get on out there, you numbskulls! And order your squads to keep a low profile, at least so the hotel doesn't notice them. Got it? Now move!"

The boys took off. Only the detectives were left in the courtyard.

"I borrowed ten marks from the porter," Emil reported. "So if the man cuts loose, we'll have enough money to follow him."

"Just tell all those kids outside to go home," Crumbagel suggested.

"You really think they'll go? They'd stay put even if Nollendorf Square exploded," said the Professor.

"There's only one solution," said Emil. "We have to change plans. Instead of trailing him with spies, we'll just have to circle him. So he knows he's trapped. All of us, on all sides."

"That's just what I was thinking," said the Professor. "We should simply change our strategy, keep pushing him until he gives himself up."

"Excellent!" shouted Gerold.

"I'm sure he'd rather cough up the money than have a hundred kids jumping and shouting after him until the whole city comes out and the police nab him," Emil added.

The others all nodded sagely. Then a bell rang out on the sidewalk, and a radiant Pony the Hat pedaled into the courtyard. "Morning, cowboys!" she called out, jumped off her bike, shook hands with Emil, the Professor, and the others, then fetched a little basket that she'd tied to the handlebars. "I brought you some coffee," she announced, "and a few English muffins! I even have a clean cup. Oh no, the handle broke off! Darn it!"

The boys had all had breakfast already. Even Emil, in Hotel Kreid. But no one wanted to dampen the little girl's enthusiasm. So they all drank the coffee from the cup without a handle and ate the English muffins like they hadn't eaten for weeks.

"Well, doesn't that hit the spot!" said Crumbagel.

"These muffins sure are crispy!" murmured the Professor as he chewed.

"Aren't they?" asked Pony. "Well, there's nothing like having a woman around the house!"

"Around the courtyard, you mean," said Gerold.

"How are things on Schumann Street?" asked Emil.

"Everyone's fine, thanks. Grandma sends her love. You better come soon, though, otherwise they'll make you eat fish for dinner every day."

"Yuck!" said Emil under his breath and made a face.

"Why yuck?" asked Middleday Junior. "Fish is good for you." Everyone looked at him in surprise, because he normally never said anything. He immediately turned red as a beet and sneaked off behind his older brother.

"Emil can't stand fish. Every time he tries it, he has to rush out of the room," Pony the Hat explained.

They continued bantering, and everyone seemed to be in a good mood. The boys were remarkably attentive. The Professor held Pony's bicycle for her. Crumbagel went and washed out the thermos and the cup. Middleday Senior cleanly folded the bag that the English muffins came in. Emil tied the basket back to the handlebars. Gerold checked the air in the tires. And Pony the Hat hopped around the courtyard, sang a little song, and chatted about this and that.

"Wait!" she shouted all of a sudden and stood still on one leg. "There's something I wanted to ask you! What is that huge crowd of kids doing on Nollendorf Square? It looks like summer camp out there!"

"They heard we were chasing a thief, and now they want to join in," explained the Professor.

Just at that moment, Gus came running into the courtyard, honked his horn, and shouted, "Come on! He's coming!" They all leapt to their feet.

"Attention everyone!" shouted the Professor. "We're going to form a circle around him. There'll be kids behind him, in front of him, to his left and to his right! Got that? You'll get further orders later on. Hup, two, three, four!"

They ran off, falling all over themselves on the way out. Pony the Hat stayed behind, a little miffed. Then she swung herself up on her little nickel-plated bicycle, murmuring, just like her grandmother, "I don't like the looks of it. I just don't like the looks of it!" and pedaled off after the boys.

The man in the bowler hat was walking out the front door of the hotel. Slowly he made his way down the steps, then turned right, toward Kleist Street. The Professor, Emil, and Gus goaded their messengers back and forth through the various groups of kids. And three minutes later, Mr. Groundsnow was surrounded.

He looked around on all sides, completely baffled. The boys were talking, laughing, and poking each other, all the while keeping pace with him. A few of them stared at the man until he got embarrassed and looked straight ahead again.

Whooosh! A ball flew by, grazing his head. He flinched, then walked faster. He tried darting into a side street. But there was already another troop of kids there coming at him.

"Man, look at his face," yelled Gus. "He always looks like he's about to sneeze."

"Walk a little in front of me," said Emil. "He doesn't need to see me just yet. He'll figure it out soon enough." Gus puffed out his chest, bulking up in front of Emil like a boxer too musclebound to walk. And Pony the Hat rode her bike alongside the procession, cheerfully ringing the bell.

The man in the bowler hat became visibly nervous. He had a vague idea of what lay in store for him and began loping forward with long strides. But it was pointless. There was no getting away from his enemies.

Suddenly he stopped and stood stock-still. Then he

spun around on his heels and walked back down the street in the opposite direction. The children all turned around, too, and began marching in reverse formation.

Then a boy—it was Crumbagel—ran in front of the man and made him stumble.

"What's your problem, you little brat?" he screamed. "I'll call the cops!"

"Oh yeah, call the cops!" Crumbagel shouted. "That's just what we've been waiting for. Go ahead, mister, call 'em!"

Mr. Groundsnow had no intention of calling the police, on the contrary. The whole situation was getting very spooky. He became truly afraid and no longer knew what to do. People were looking out their windows. Salesclerks and customers were coming out of the stores, asking what was going on. If the police showed up now, he was done for.

Then the thief had an idea. He noticed a bank on the corner. He broke through the chain of children, rushed to the door of the bank, and vanished inside.

The Professor bounded to the door and shouted, "Gus and I will go in after him! Emil will stay here until it's time. Wait for Gus to honk his horn. Then, Emil, you come in with ten other boys. Pick out the right ones now. This is going to be tricky!"

The Professor and Gus disappeared through the door.

Emil's heart was beating wildly. This was it! He called over Crumbagel, Gerold, the Middleday brothers, and a few others, and instructed everyone else, the army of kids, to scatter.

The children walked away from the bank building, but not very far. No way were they were going to miss what happened next.

Pony the Hat asked a boy to hold her bicycle and went over to Emil.

"I'm here," she said. "Chin up, Emil. This is it. My God, are my nerves ever shot."

"And you think mine aren't?" asked Emil.

CHAPTER FOURTEEN

PINS HAVE THEIR USES

GUS AND THE PROFESSOR WALKED INTO THE BANK AND SAW the man in the bowler already standing at a counter marked "Deposits and Withdrawals." He was waiting impatiently for the teller to get off the phone.

The Professor went and stood next to the thief and watched him like a Pointer. Gus stood behind him with one hand in his pants pocket, ready to honk the horn.

The teller came to the window and asked the Professor what he could do for him. The Professor answered, "I'm sorry, but this gentleman here was before me."

"Yes?" the teller asked Mr. Groundsnow.

"Would you please change this hundred-mark bill into two fifties," he asked, digging into his pocket, "and give me the forty marks in one- and five-mark coins?" He laid a hundred-mark bill and two twenty-mark bills on the counter.

The teller took the three bills and walked over to the safe.

"Just a moment!" the Professor shouted. "That money is stolen!"

"Whaaat?" the teller asked, astonished, and turned around. His coworkers, who were sitting and crunching numbers in the other departments, jumped out their seats as if a snake had bitten them.

"That money doesn't belong to this man. He stole it from a friend of mine, and now he wants to change it so that no one can prove it," the Professor explained.

"Never in my life have I witnessed such insolence!" said Mr. Groundsnow. "Please excuse me," he said to the teller, then turned to the Professor and smacked him on the head.

"That won't change anything," said the Professor and slugged Groundsnow in the stomach so hard that the man had to hold onto the counter. And now Gus honked his horn three times as loud as he could. The curious bank employees all jumped up and ran to see what was happening.

The bank manager stormed out of his office like a hornet.

And then—ten boys came running in through the front door, Emil at their helm, and surrounded the man in the bowler hat.

"What on earth are these kids doing here?" shouted the manager.

"These little delinquents claim that the money I just asked your teller to change for me was stolen, by me, from one of them!" Mr. Groundsnow explained, trembling with anger.

"It's true!" yelled Emil and ran up to the counter. "He stole a hundred-mark bill and two twenties from me. Yesterday afternoon. In the train on the way from New Town to Berlin! While I was sleeping!"

"Sure, but can you prove it?" asked the teller.

"I've been in Berlin for a week and yesterday I was in the city from morning to night," said the thief with a polite smile.

"That's a lie!" shouted Emil, practically in tears with anger.

"Can you prove that this man was on the train with you?" asked the bank manager.

"Of course he can't," said the thief nonchalantly.

"If you were sitting alone with him in the train, then there can't have been any witnesses," one of the bank employees pointed out. Emil's friends looked shocked.

"But there were!" shouted Emil, "I do have a witness! Mrs. Jacob from Great Greenow. She was in the same compartment with us, then she got out. She asked me to say hello to Mr. Squatneck from New Town."

"It seems you'll have to supply an alibi," said the bank manager to the thief. "Can you do that?"

"Of course," he said. "I'm staying across the way in Hotel Kreid . . ."

"But he only checked in there last night," said Gus. "I've been working undercover as a bellhop there. I know."

The bank employees all chuckled and became even more curious about the boys.

"I think it's best if we hold onto the money here for the moment, Mr . . . ?" said the manager and tore off a sheet of paper from a notepad in order to write down the name and address.

"Mr. Groundsnow!" shouted Emil.

The man in the bowler hat laughed out loud and said, "There, you see, the boy has mistaken me for someone else. My name is Mueller."

"That's a baldfaced lie! He told me in the train his name was Groundsnow," Emil shouted furiously.

"Do you have an I.D.?" asked the teller.

"Unfortunately not on me," said the thief. "But if you don't mind waiting a few minutes, I'll go and get it from the hotel."

"The guy's a pathological liar! And it's my money. And I need to have it back," shouted Emil.

"Well, even if that's true, young man," the teller explained, "it's not so simple. How can you prove that the money is yours? Is your name written on it? Or did you happen to write down the serial numbers?"

"Of course not," said Emil. "Do you leave the house expecting to get robbed? But it's still my money. Don't you understand? My mother gave it to me to give to my grandmother, who lives at 15 Schumann Street."

"Was there anything strange about the bills themselves? One of the corners ripped off, for example?"

"No. I really don't know."

"Gentlemen, I give you my word. The money really does belong to me. I am certainly not one to rip off little kids."

"Wait!" Emil shouted suddenly and jumped into the air, he was so relieved. "Wait! In the train, I pinned the money to the inside of my jacket. So there should be pinholes in the three bills!"

The teller held the money up to the light. The thief's breath caught in his throat.

He took a step back. The bank director nervously drummed his fingers on the counter.

"The boy is right!" cried the teller, pale with excitement. "There really are pinholes in all three bills!"

"And here's the pin that made them," said Emil, and proudly laid the pin on the counter. "I even pricked myself with it."

At that the thief spun around on his heels, shoved, then pushed over, the boys on either side of him, ran across the room, threw open the door, and was gone.

"After him!" shouted the bank director.

Everyone ran to the door.

When they got to the street, the thief was there, surrounded on all sides by at least twenty boys. They clutched his legs. They hung from his arms. They tore at his jacket. He waved his arms around like mad, but the boys wouldn't let go.

Then a police officer came running to the scene. Pony the Hat had gone on her little bike to fetch him. The bank manager insisted that he arrest the man, whose name was either Groundsnow or Mueller or both, since he was, in all likelihood, a train robber.

The teller took the rest of the day off, grabbed the money and the pin, and joined them. Well, it sure was some procession! The policeman and the bank manager, with the thief in between them, and behind them ninety to a hundred kids! Walking all together to the police station.

Pony the Hat rode her little nickel-plated bicycle alongside them. She nodded at her overjoyed cousin Emil and shouted, "Emil, good on you! I'm riding back home to tell them the whole story!"

The boy nodded back at her and said, "I'll be home for lunch! Say hello to everyone!"

Then Pony the Hat shouted one more thing: "You know what you all look like? Like a whole school on a field trip!" And with a loud ring of her bell she turned the corner.

CHAPTER FIFTEEN

EMIL VISITS POLICE HEADQUARTERS

THE PROCESSION MARCHED TO THE NEAREST POLICE STATION. The policeman informed the sheriff there of the incident. Emil filed his report. Then he had to give his date and place of birth, his full name, and residence. The sheriff wrote everything down. In ink.

"And what is your name?" he asked the thief.

"Herbert Kiessling," said the guy.

At that, the boys—Emil, Gus, and the Professor—all had to laugh. And the bank teller, who had handed over the one hundred and forty marks to the sheriff, laughed with them.

"Man, what a nut!" exclaimed Gus. "First he says his name's Groundsnow. Then it's Mueller. And now Kiessling! I can't wait to find out what his real name is!"

"Quiet!" growled the sheriff. "We'll find that out soon enough."

Mr. Groundsnow-Mueller-Kiessling then told the sheriff his current address, Hotel Kreid. Then his birthdate and home town. He claimed he didn't have an ID.

"And where were you before yesterday?" asked the sheriff.

"In Great Greenow," the thief replied.

"He's probably lying again," said the Professor.

"Quiet!" growled the patrolman. "We'll find that out soon enough."

The bank teller asked whether he could go. Then his details, too, were taken down. He gave Emil a friendly pat on the shoulder and took off.

"Mr. Kiessling," the sheriff began. "Did you steal a hundred and forty marks from the New Town schoolboy Emil Tabletoe in the train to Berlin yesterday?"

"I did," the thief said gloomily. "I don't know why. It just came over me. The boy was lying there in the corner, sleeping, when the envelope fell out of his pocket. I picked it up and had a look inside. And since I was broke at the time . . ."

"That's a lie!" exclaimed Emil. "The money was pinned to my jacket pocket. There's no way it fell out!"

"And he couldn't have needed it that much, otherwise he wouldn't have had the whole amount on him still. He had at least enough of his own money for a taxi, Eggs Benedict, and beer," the Professor pointed out.

"Quiet!" growled the patrolman. "We'll find that out soon enough."

And he wrote down everything everyone said.

"Do you think you could possibly let me go, Officer?" the thief asked, positively oozing politeness. "I admitted the crime, after all. And you know where I'm staying. You see, I'm in Berlin on business, and I have some errands to run."

"Oh, you're a riot!" said the sheriff with a straight face. He called police headquarters and asked them to send a car over; he had a train robber in custody.

"So when do I get my money back?" asked a worried Emil.

"They'll give it you at headquarters," said the sheriff. "You'll all go over there now, and everything will get sorted out."

"Hey!" whispered Gus. "They're taking you to head-quarters in a paddy wagon!"

"Baloney!" said the sheriff. "You got any money at all, Tabletoe?"

"I sure do," said Emil. "The guys passed the hat around yesterday. And the porter at Hotel Kreid lent me ten marks."

"A bunch of regular detectives, huh? Wise guys!" growled the sheriff. But it sounded like a very friendly growl.

"Listen up, Tabletoe. You take the subway to Alexander Place and check in with Sheriff Lurje. You'll figure out the rest once you're there. And you'll get your money back, too."

"Can I go give the porter his ten marks back first?" Emil asked.

"Of course."

A few minutes later the police van arrived. And Mr. Groundsnow-Mueller-Kiessling had to get in. The sheriff handed over the written report, the hundred and forty marks, and the pin to a police officer who was sitting in the cab. Then the paddy wagon trundled away. The children standing on the street screamed after the thief. But he didn't flinch. Probably he was too proud, getting to ride in his own car and all.

Emil shook the sheriff's hand and thanked him. The Professor informed the children who had been waiting in front of the station that Emil would be getting his money at police headquarters and that the chase was now over. Then the children, large packs of them, all wandered home. Only the close circle of friends went with Emil to the Hotel and to Nollendorf Square subway station. He asked them to call little Tuesday in the afternoon and let him know how everything went. And he really hoped to see them all again before he went back to New Town. He wanted to thank them all from the bottom of his heard for helping him out. And they would get their money back, of course.

"Just try giving us that money back and I'll clobber you!" exclaimed Gus. "By the way, we still have to box. Over that weird suit of yours."

"Oh, man!" said Emil and grabbed Gus's and the

Professor's hands. "I'm in such a great mood! Let's forget about the boxing match. It would break my heart to have to deck you."

"You couldn't deck me even if you were in a bad mood, you dork!" yelled Gus.

Then the three rode to police headquarters at Alexander Place. They had to walk through a lot of hallways and past countless rooms before finding Officer Lurje, the criminal sheriff. He was having breakfast. Emil introduced himself.

"Aha!" said Officer Lurje, chewing. "Emil Tabletop. Kid Detective. Heard about it on the phone. The police chief is waiting. He wants to talk to you. Come with me!

"The name is Tabletoe," Emil corrected him.

"Six of one, half dozen of the other," said Officer Lurje, taking another bite of his bagel.

"We'll wait for you here," said the Professor. Gus called after Emil, "Make it quick, dude! When I see someone eating, I always get hungry!"

Officer Lurje wandered through a number of corridors, left, right, left again. Then he knocked on a door. A voice called, "Come in!" Lurje cracked open the door and said, chewing, "The kid detective is here, Chief. Emil Mistletoe."

"My name is Tabletoe!" Emil insisted.

"Well, that's a nice name, too," said Officer Lurje and shoved Emil so hard, he tumbled into the room.

The police chief was a friendly man. Emil had to sit

in a comfy chair and tell him the whole robber story in detail from start to finish. At the end, the police chief stood up and announced, "Well, I suppose I should give you your money back now."

"Thank God!" Emil gave a huge sigh of relief and put the money in his pocket. And he was especially careful with it.

"Just don't let it get stolen again!"

"No way! I'm taking it straight to Grandma!"

"Right! I almost forgot. I'll need your address here in Berlin. Will you be here for the next couple of days?"

"I hope so," said Emil. "I'm staying at 15 Schumann Street. The Heimbold residence. That's my uncle's last name. My aunt's, too, actually."

"You boys did an excellent job," said the police chief, lighting a fat cigar.

"Yep, the team functioned like a well-oiled machine, it's true!" replied Emil enthusiastically. "Gus and his horn, the Professor, little Tuesday, Crumbagel, and the Middleday brothers—everybody. It was so awesome working with them. Most of all with the Professor. What a whiz!"

"Well, you're not exactly pea-brained either," said the police chief, letting out a puff of smoke.

"There's something else I wanted to ask you, Officer," said Emil. "What will happen to Groundsnow, or whatever the thief's name is?"

"We took him over to identify him. He'll be pho-

tographed and fingerprinted. Then we'll compare his picture and prints with the ones we have in our database."

"What's that?"

"That's where we keep files on everyone who's been arrested, and also for keeping evidence—footprints, things like that—on criminals we haven't caught yet and are still looking for. It's possible, after all, that the man who stole your money committed other robberies and burglaries long before pickpocketing you. Right?"

"That's true. I didn't even think about it!"

"Just a sec," said the friendly police chief and picked up the ringing phone. "By all means," he said into the speaker, "Yes, a very interesting case . . . just come into my office." Then he hung up and said to Emil, "A couple of fellows from the newspaper will be here in a moment to interview you."

"What does that mean?" asked Emil.

"That means they're going to ask you some questions."

"Unbelievable!" exclaimed Emil. "So I'm going to be in the newspaper, too?"

"Probably," said the police chief. "Schoolkids who catch robbers usually become famous."

There was a knock at the door. Then four gentlemen came into the room. The police chief shook their hands and briefly told them Emil's story. The four men diligently wrote everything down.

"This is great!" said one of the reporters at the end. "Country boy turns detective!"

"So are you putting him on the payroll, Chief?" said another and laughed.

"What I don't understand is why you didn't just tell the police in the first place," asked a third reporter.

Emil felt a chill run down his spine. He thought about Officer Jeschke in New Town and about his dream. Now he was really in for it.

"Good question . . ." said the police chief.

Emil shrugged his shoulders and said, "Oh, all right! It's because back in New Town I painted a moustache on the statue of Grand Duke Charles. I painted his nose red, too. Please don't arrest me, Mr. Police Chief!"

At that, instead of scowling, the five men all laughed. The police chief exclaimed, "But Emil, we couldn't possibly put our best detective behind bars!"

"No? Really? Wow, does that ever make me happy!" the boy said with a sigh of relief.

Then he went to one of the reporters and said, "Don't you remember me?"

"No," replied the man.

"You paid for my ticket yesterday on the streetcar when I didn't have the money."

"That's right!" said the man. "Now I remember. You wanted to know my address so you could return the dime."

"Would you like it back now?" asked Emil and pulled ten pennies out of his pants pocket.

"Don't bother," said the man. "You even introduced yourself."

"Of course," said Emil. "I always do that. Tabletoe's the name. Emil Tabletoe."

"And my name's Kästner," said the journalist, and they shook hands.

"Amazing!" said the police chief. "Old pals!"

"Say, Emil," said Mr. Kästner, "why don't you come over to the newspaper with me. We can go for cake and ice cream on the way."

"All right, but it's on me!" said Emil.

"What a hotshot!" The men all laughed with delight.

"No. Please. Let me pay for it!" said Mr. Kästner.

"Well, thanks," said Emil. "But the Professor and Gus are waiting for me outside."

"They'll join us, of course," said Mr. Kästner.

The other journalists still had a lot of questions for Emil. He answered them all in detail, and they wrote down even more notes.

"Is the thief a first-timer?" one of the men asked.

"I don't think so," replied the police chief. "We may be in for another big surprise. But wait an hour or so, gentleman, then give me a call."

They all said goodbye to each other. And Emil went with Mr. Kästner back to Officer Lurje. He was still eating. "Ah, the little Tiptoe!" he said.

"Tabletoe," said Emil.

Then Mr. Kästner packed Emil, Gus, and the Professor into a cab and rode with them to an ice cream shop. On the way, Gus honked his horn, and everyone laughed when Mr. Kästner jumped in surprise. The boys were all in high spirits at the ice cream shop. They had cherry pie smothered in whipped cream and talked about this and that—about the council meeting on Nikolsburg Square, the car chase, the night in the hotel, Gus dressed up as a bellhop, and the commotion in the bank. At the end Mr. Kästner said, "You guys are geniuses!"

All three were suddenly very proud of themselves, so they each had another slice of pie.

Afterwards Gus and the Professor got on the bus. Emil promised to call little Tuesday in the afternoon, then headed with Mr. Kästner for the editorial office.

The newspaper building was enormous, almost as big as the police headquarters on Alexander Place. The halls were filled with people scurrying and running back and forth as if an obstacle race were going on.

They entered a room where a beautiful blonde woman was sitting at a typewriter. Mr. Kästner paced back and forth across the room and dictated what Emil had told him to the woman. Sometimes he stopped all of a sudden and asked Emil, "Is that right?" When Emil nodded, Mr. Kästner continued dictating.

Then he made a phone call to the police chief.

"What's that you say?" shouted Mr. Kästner. "Why . . . why that's amazing! . . . But I shouldn't say anything to him? . . . Oh, that too? . . . I am so happy . . . Thanks a million! . . . This'll be great . . ."

He hung up, looked at Emil as if he were seeing him

for the first time, and said, "Emil, come with me. You're going to get your picture taken!"

"Uh, okay . . ." said Emil, a little surprised. But he went along with it. He took the elevator with Mr. Kästner three floors up to a brightly lit room with a lot of windows. He combed his hair, and then his picture was taken.

After that, Mr. Kästner took him along to the composing room—was that ever a racket! like a thousand typewriters going at once!—and gave a man the pages that the beautiful woman had typed. He said he would be coming right back, that this was something very important, and that he just needed to send the boy off to his grandmother's first.

Then they took the elevator to the ground floor and walked out to the street. Mr. Kästner hailed a cab, put Emil in it, gave money to the driver—although the boy didn't want him to—and said, "Please take my little friend here to 15 Schumann Street."

They shook hands, and Mr. Kästner said, "Give my greetings to your mother when you get home. She must be a wonderful woman."

"She sure is," said Emil.

"And one more thing," shouted Mr. Kästner as the cab was pulling away. "Read the newspaper tomorrow! You're in for a big surprise!"

Emil turned around and waved. And Mr. Kästner waved back.

Then the cab zoomed around the corner.

CHAPTER SIXTEEN

THE POLICE CHIEF SENDS HIS REGARDS

THE TAXI WAS ALREADY ON UNDER THE LINDENS BOULEVARD when Emil knocked three times against the window. The car stopped, and the boy asked, "We're probably getting close, right?"

"Not far at all," said the man.

"Well, I'm really sorry to bother you," said Emil, "But I have to go back to Emperor Avenue first. To Café Josty. I left a bouquet of flowers there for my grandmother. And my suitcase. Do you mind?"

"Why should I mind? You got money in case what I have here doesn't cover it?"

"I do. And I really need to get those flowers."

"Fine with me," said the man and took a left turn, then drove through Brandenburg Gate and down along the green and shady Tiergarten Park to Nollendorf Square. Emil thought it looked much nicer and a lot less dangerous now that things were back to normal. But he still checked his suit coat pocket to make sure the money was there. Then they drove down to the other end of Motz Street, turned right, and stopped in front of Café Josty.

Emil got out, went up to the counter and asked the lady if she would please give him his suitcase and flowers. She did, and he thanked her, then got back into the taxi and said, "Well, Mr. Cab Driver, let's go to Grandma's!"

They turned around and drove all the way back, across the Spree River and through a lot of really old streets with gray buildings. The boy would have liked to get a better look at the neighborhood. But it was like someone had put a spell on him. The suitcase kept falling over. And whenever it did stay put for a few moments, the wind would come blowing through and make the white paper around the flowers flutter and tear. Emil had to watch out that the bouquet did not simply go flying out the window.

The driver put on the brakes. The taxi stopped. They were at 15 Schumann Street.

"Here we are then!" said Emil and got out. "Do I owe you any money?"

"No. But I owe you thirty cents."

"Keep it!" said Emil, "and buy yourself a couple of cigars!"

"Chewing tobacco, son, chewing tobacco," the driver said and drove off.

Then Emil walked up to the fourth floor and rang the Heimbolds' doorbell. He heard a loud scream from behind the door. Then it opened, and there was his grandmother. She grabbed Emil by the sleeve, and simultaneously kissed him on the left cheek and cuffed him on the right. Then she pulled him by the hair into the apartment, crying, "Oh, you rascal, you little rascal!"

"We've been hearing great things about you," said Aunt Martha, smiling, and shook his hand. Pony the Hat was wearing one of her mother's aprons. She held out her elbow to him and squeaked, "Careful! My hands are dripping. I'm washing dishes. A woman's work is never done, is it?"

They all moved to the living room. Emil had to sit on the sofa. Grandma and Aunt Martha both looked at him as if he were an original Rembrandt.

"You got the money?" asked Pony the Hat.

"Of course I do!" said Emil and pulled three bills out of his pocket. He gave the one hundred and twenty marks to his grandmother and said, "Here, Grandma, here's the money. And Mom sends her love. And she says not to be mad that she couldn't send anything the last few months, but business wasn't so great. So that's why she's sending more than usual now."

"Well, thank you very much, my dear," the old woman said. She gave the twenty-mark bill back to him and said, "There, that's for you! For being such a clever detective!"

"I'm sorry, but I can't take it. Anyway I already have twenty marks that Mom gave me."

"Emil, listen to your grandmother. Keep the money and put it in your pocket."

"No, I won't do it."

"For God's sake!" cried Pony the Hat. "You sure wouldn't need to ask me twice."

"I really don't want to."

"Either you take the money, or you'll make me so mad I'll get rheumatism," said Grandma.

"Emil, put the money away," said Aunt Martha and tucked the twenty marks into his pocket.

"Well, if you all insist," moaned Emil. "Anyway, thanks, Grandma."

"I should thank you, I should thank you," she replied and patted him on his head.

Then Emil gave her the bouquet of flowers. Pony went to get a vase. But when they unwrapped the paper, they didn't know whether to laugh or cry.

"Look, dried salad!" said Pony.

"No wonder. They haven't had any water since yesterday afternoon," Emil explained sadly. "But when Mom and I bought them yesterday at Stamnitzen's, they were completely fresh."

"I believe it, I believe it," said Grandma and stuck the withered flowers in the water.

"Maybe they'll come back," said Aunt Martha. "Well, it's time to have lunch. Your uncle won't be home until dinner. Pony, would you set the table?"

"Sure thing," said the little girl. "Hey Emil, what are we having for lunch?"

"How should I know?"

"What's your favorite dish?"

"Macaroni and ham."

"See? You do know what we're having for lunch!"

It's true that Emil had just had macaroni and ham the day before. But first of all, it's not hard to eat your favorite dish every day. And second, Emil had the feeling that a whole week had gone by since he had left his mother in New Town. He attacked the macaroni as if he had a plate of Mr. Groundsnow-Mueller-Kiessling in front of him.

When they finished eating, Emil and the Hat went outside for a bit because the boy wanted to try Pony's little nickel-plated bicycle. Grandma took a nap on the couch. And Aunt Martha baked an apple pie in the oven. Her apple pie was legendary in the whole family.

Emil pedaled down Schumann Street. And Pony the Hat ran after him, holding onto the seat. She said she had to, otherwise her cousin would go flying off. Then he had to get off the bike, and she rode circles and crazy eights around him.

Then a policeman carrying a briefcase came up to them and asked, "Hey kids, does the Heimbold family live here in number 15?"

"Yep," said Pony, "that's us. Be right with you, Captain." She went to put her bicycle away in the cellar.

"Why, did something bad happen?" asked Emil. He couldn't help thinking about Officer Jeschke.

"Oh no, not at all. Are you the schoolboy Emil Tabletoe?"

"I am."

"Well, you should be congratulated!"

"Hey, who won the lottery?" asked Pony, who was just returning.

But the officer said nothing; he simply walked up the steps. Aunt Martha led him into the living room. Grandma woke up, sat up, and seemed very curious. Emil and Pony stood by the table with bated breath.

"Here's the story," said the officer, opening his briefcase. "The thief apprehended this morning by the schoolboy Emil Tabletoe is identical to a bank robber from Hanover for whom an arrest warrant was issued four weeks ago. This robber has stolen a great deal of money. We indicted him, and he confessed to the crime. Most of the money was subsequently found hidden in the lining of his jacket. All in thousand-mark bills."

"Get outta here!" said Pony the Hat.

"Two weeks ago," the policeman continued, "the bank offered a reward to anyone who caught the man. And since you," he turned to Emil, "did the job, you'll get that reward. The police chief is very happy that your hard work will be compensated. He sends his regards, by the way."

Emil made a bow.

The officer then took a wad of money out of his briefcase and counted it onto the table. When he finished, Aunt Martha, who was paying close attention, whispered, "A thousand marks!"

"Whoa!" exclaimed Pony. "That's insane!"

Grandma signed a receipt. Then the officer left, but not before Aunt Martha could give him a big glass of cherry brandy from Uncle Robert's cabinet.

Emil took a seat next to his grandmother. He was speechless. The old woman put her arm around him and shook her head. "I can hardly believe it," she said, "I can hardly believe it."

Pony the Hat got up on a chair, raised her arms like a music director in front of a chorus, and sang, "Now let's invite, now let's invite the other boys over for a party!"

"Yeah," said Emil, "that would be good. But most of all . . . actually, couldn't . . . what do you think . . . couldn't Mom come to Berlin, too?"

CHAPTER SEVENTEEN

MRS. TABLETOE
IS IN A TIZZY

THE NEXT MORNING IN NEW TOWN, MRS. WORTH, THE baker's wife, rang the doorbell of Mrs. Tabletoe, the hairdresser. "Hello, Mrs. Tabletoe," she said. "How are things?"

"Good morning, Mrs. Worth, I'm terribly worried! My son still hasn't written a word. Every time the bell rings, I think it's the postman. Would you like me to do your hair?"

"No thanks. I just wanted to stop by and, well, I have a message for you."

"Yes?"

"Emil says to say hello, and . . ."

"Good heavens! What happened to him? Where is he? What do you know?" shouted Mrs. Tabletoe. She was terribly upset and anxiously held up both her hands.

"But he's fine, dear. Very fine, in fact. He caught a thief. Just imagine! And the police gave him a thousand marks as a reward. What do you say to that? Hmm? And they want you to come to Berlin on the afternoon train."

"But how do you know all this?"

"You sister Martha just called me at my shop. I talked to Emil for a bit as well. And you really should go! Now that you have so much money, it shouldn't be a problem."

"Well, well . . . I suppose . . ." murmured a distraught Mrs. Tabletoe. "A thousand marks? For catching a thief? What on earth was he thinking? All he ever does is get into trouble!"

"But it was worth it! A thousand marks is a lot of money after all."

"You can have your thousand marks!"

"Well, worse things have happened. So, are you going to Berlin?"

"Of course! I won't have a moment's rest until I see that boy again."

"Well, then have a good trip! And have fun!"

"Thank you, Mrs. Worth," said the hairdresser and closed the door, shaking her head.

That afternoon, sitting on the train to Berlin, Emil's mother was in for an even greater surprise. Across from her a man was reading the paper. She looked nervously from one corner to the other, counted the telephone poles going by outside the window, and would have liked nothing more than to get out and push the train from behind. It was going much too slowly for her.

While she was fidgeting and turning her head this way and that, her eyes landed on the newspaper.

"Oh my God!" she shouted and ripped the paper out

of the man's hands. The man thought the woman had suddenly lost her mind and got scared.

"There! There!" she stammered. "This here . . . that's my son!" She poked with her finger at a photograph on the front page.

"You don't say!" said the man with relief. "So you're the mother of Emil Tabletoe? You have a gem of a son. Hats off to you, Mrs. Tabletoe, hats off to you!"

"Well," said the hairdresser. "You can leave your hat on, mister!" And she began to read the article. It had an enormous headline:

BOY DETECTIVE!
HUNDREDS OF BERLIN KIDS CATCH CRIMINAL

Then came a long and gripping report about everything Emil had experienced from the New Town train station to the police headquarters in Berlin. The blood drained from Mrs. Tabletoe's face. And the newspaper trembled as if the wind were blowing through the compartment, even though the windows were shut. The man could hardly wait for her to finish reading the article. But it was quite long and took up almost the whole front page. Right in the middle was Emil's picture.

At last she put the paper down, looked at the man, and said, "Hardly does he leave the house than he gets into trouble. If I told him once I told him a thousand times to keep an eye on that hundred and forty marks! How could he be so careless? He knows perfectly well we don't have money for other people to steal!"

"But he got sleepy. Maybe the thief even hypnotized him. It can happen," said the man. "But don't you think it's great how those boys handled the situation? They were amazing! Absolutely brilliant!"

"I suppose you're right," said Mrs. Tabletoe, flattered. "He certainly is a smart boy, my son is. Always the top student in school and a hard worker, besides. But what if something had happened to him! It makes my hair stand on end, even though it's all over now. No, I can't let him travel by himself ever again. I'd die of fear."

"Does he look just like he does in the picture?" asked the man.

Mrs. Tabletoe looked at the photograph again and said, "Yes. Just like that. What do you think?"

"He's great!" exclaimed the man. "What a guy. He's got success written all over his face."

"But he should have sat up straight for the picture," Emil's mother griped. "His jacket is all wrinkled. He should always button it up before he sits down. But he never listens!"

"Ha, with faults like that . . . !" laughed the man.

"It's true, he doesn't really have any faults, my Emil," said Mrs. Tabletoe. She choked up and had to blow her nose . . .

Then the man got off the train.

He let her keep the newspaper, and she read Emil's story over and over on the way to Frederick Street Station. Eleven times total.

When she arrived in Berlin, Emil was standing on the platform. He was wearing his good suit in her honor. He gave her a big hug and exclaimed, "So, what do you think, huh?"

"Don't let it go to your head, you oaf!"

"Oh, Mrs. Tabletoe," he said and took her arm in his, "I'm so happy you came!"

"Well, I can see catching criminals hasn't done your suit much good," said his mother. But she did not sound very angry.

"If you want, I can get a new suit."

"From whom?"

"A department store wants to give the Professor and Gus and me new suits and put ads in the newspapers about how detectives like us only buy our suits from them. It's marketing. Get it?"

"Yes, I get it."

"But we'll probably say no, even though we could each get a soccer ball instead of a boring suit," Emil boasted. "We think all the commotion they're making about us is pretty ridiculous, you know. The grown-ups are welcome to do whatever they want. They're weird anyway. But kids shouldn't bother."

"Bravo!" said his mother.

"Uncle Robert locked the money away. A thousand marks. Isn't that cool? The first thing we'll buy is an electric salon dryer for you. And a winter coat with a fur lining. As for me? I'll have to think first. Maybe I'll get a soccer ball. Or a camera. We'll see."

"I was thinking it might be better to put the money away in a savings account. I'm sure you'll have a need for it someday in the future."

"No, you'll get the dryer and the warm coat. We can put away what's left, if you want."

"Well, we can talk about it later," said Emil's mother and gave his arm a squeeze.

"Did you know that all the newspapers have pictures of me in them? And long articles about me?"

"I read one of them in the train. I was very upset at first, Emil! Did you get hurt?"

"Not at all. It was awesome! Well, I'll tell you all about it later. But first you have to meet my friends."

"Where are they?"

"Over on Schumann Street. At Aunt Martha's. She made an apple pie yesterday, and we invited the whole gang over. They're sitting at home making a big commotion."

There really was a lot going on at the Heimbold residence. Everyone was there: Gus, the Professor, Crumbagel, the Middleday brothers, Gerold, Freddie the Great, Truegut, little Tuesday, and the rest. There were hardly enough chairs to go around. With a big pitcher in hand, Pony the Hat ran from one to the other, serving hot chocolate. Aunt Martha's apple pie was poetry in a pan! And Grandma sat on the sofa, beaming and looking ten years younger.

When Emil and his mom came in, they all said hello and introduced themselves. Mrs. Tabletoe shook each boy's hand in turn and thanked them for having helped her son. "So look," Emil announced, "we're not accepting the suits or the soccer balls. They're not going to make commercials out of us. What do you think of that?"

"Right on!" shouted Gus and honked his horn so loud that Aunt Martha's flowerpots rattled.

Then Grandma struck her spoon a few times against her gold-colored coffee cup, stood up, and said, "Listen up, troopers. I want to make a speech. Now, don't let this business go to your heads! Personally, I don't think what you did was so special. Other people may be driving you all bananas. But I'm not buying it. No, I just don't buy it!"

The children fell completely silent and even stopped chewing.

"A hundred children chasing a thief and catching him like that," Grandma went on. "Well, that's not hard at all. Does it bother you that I'm saying this, boys? There's one of you here, though, who would have been very happy to go tiptoeing after Mr. Groundsnow. He'd have liked nothing more than to snoop around the hotel dressed up as a bell-hop. But he stayed at home because he took on a responsibility. That's right, because he had a responsibility."

Everyone looked over at little Tuesday. His face had gone brick-red, he was so embarrassed.

"That's right, that's right! I'm talking about little Tuesday," said the old woman. "He spent two days sitting by the phone. He knew what his duty was. And he did it, even if he didn't particularly enjoy it. That was amazing, you understand? What he did was amazing! He should be

an example to all of you! So let's all stand up and shout:
Hurray for little Tuesday!"

The boys jumped to their feet. Pony the Hat held her
hands to her mouth like a trumpet. Aunt Martha and
Emil's mother came out of the kitchen. And everyone
shouted, "Hurray for little Tuesday! Hurray! Hurray!"

Then they all sat down again. And little Tuesday took
a deep breath and said, "Thanks, guys. But you're making
a big deal out of it. You would've done the same thing, I'm
sure! A real boy does what he has to do!"

Pony the Hat held up the big pitcher and yelled, "Hey
folks, who needs more to drink? It's time to toast Emil!"

CHAPTER EIGHTEEN

IS THERE A MORAL TO THE STORY?

TOWARD EVENING THE BOYS ALL LEFT. AND EMIL HAD TO swear up and down that he and Pony the Hat would be at the Professor's the following afternoon. Then Mr. Heimbold came home and they had dinner. Afterwards he gave the thousand marks to his sister-in-law, Mrs. Tabletoe, and advised her to put the money in the bank.

"I was already planning to do just that," said the hairdresser.

"No!" cried Emil. "You're taking all the fun out of it. Mom should get herself an electric hair dryer and a fur-lined coat. What's with you people? The money belongs to me. I can do with it what I want, can't I?"

"You can't do anything with it," explained Uncle Robert. "You're a minor. It's up to your mother to decide what to do with the money."

Emil got up from the table and walked over to the window.

"Come on, Heimbold! Don't be such a dork!" said

Pony the Hat to her father. "Can't you see how happy it would make Emil to give his mom a present? You grown-ups can be such numbskulls sometimes!"

"Of course she'll get herself a hair dryer and a coat," said Grandma. "But whatever's left will go into the bank. Right, Emil?"

"That's right," said Emil. "Is that okay with you, Mom?"

"If you say so, you wealthy man!"

"We'll go shopping first thing in the morning. Pony, you're coming with me!" exclaimed a very satisfied Emil.

"You think I'm staying here and twiddling my thumbs?" said his cousin. "But you have to buy something for yourself, too. Of course your mom should get her hair dryer, but you should get a bike of your own, so you don't keep riding mine around and messing it up."

"Emil," Mrs. Tabletoe asked worriedly, "did you break Pony's bicycle?"

"Oh Mom! I just raised her seat a little. She likes to monkey around and ride with it all the way down so she looks like a motorbike racer."

"You're the monkey!" yelled Pony. "If you mess with my bike one more time, I'll never talk to you again, got that?"

"If you weren't a girl and as skinny as a rake, I'd pop you one. I really don't feel like being in a bad mood today, but what I buy or don't buy with my money is none of your business." And Emil sullenly shoved both his fists into his trouser pockets.

"Don't argue, don't fight, just scratch each other's eyes out," said Grandma, trying to calm them down. And the whole matter was dropped.

Later, Uncle Robert went out to walk the dog. The Heimbolds did not actually have a dog, but that's what Pony called it whenever her father went out at night for a beer.

Then Grandma and the two women and Pony the Hat and Emil sat in the living room and talked about the past few days, which had been so exciting.

"Well, maybe there's a moral to the story," said Aunt Martha.

"Of course," said Emil. "One lesson I've already learned: You shouldn't trust anyone."

Then his mother said, "And I learned that you should never let your children travel alone."

"Baloney!" barked Grandma. "You've got it all wrong. All wrong!"

"Baloney, baloney, baloney!" sang Pony the Hat and rode her chair across the room.

"You mean to say, the story has no moral?" asked Aunt Martha.

"Of course it does," said Grandma.

"What is it then?" the others all asked in unison.å

"Don't send cash—use traveler's checks!" Grandma started to growl again, then just giggled like a music box.

"Yippee!" shouted Pony the Hat and rode her chair into the bedroom.

THE END

TRANSLATOR'S NOTE

This is at least the third translation of *Emil and the Detectives* into English, and the first to be commissioned for a twenty-first-century American reader. To that end I have attempted to render the story—which is as universal as it is local—into a contemporary, colloquial American idiom. This was at times quite challenging, given that the language and details of the original are so tightly woven into the fabric of everyday life in Germany in the 1920s. So if sometimes the characters do things that seem odd, keep in mind that they were doing them over seventy years ago.

I have translated places names into their English equivalents. If you travel to Berlin today, you will find them all still there; only instead of Nollendorf Square, for instance, you'll find *Nollendorfplatz*, and Frederick Street Train Station is actually known as *Bahnhof Friedrichstrasse*. I have also translated most of the last names in order to preserve in English at least some of the humor of the German. Emil, for instance, is originally Emil *Tischbein* —which could easily be someone's last name—but because it also means, literally, "table leg," I wanted to find an equivalent that would sound believable in English, somewhat quirky on its own, and also allow me to accommodate Officer Lurje's jokes. I hope it works.

I would like to thank Joseph Farias-Eisner, Paul Hockenos, and Margaret Viola for their helpful comments on different drafts of the translation. I dedicate this translation to my nieces and nephews, Casper, Christina, Bobby, Michael, and Beth.